Nuclear Revenge

A WW2 German weapon 75 years in the making

By J. T. Skye

Copyright © 2020 by J. T. Skye

Amazon Kindle Edition

Discover other stories at

JTSkye.com

Disclaimer

This is a work of fiction. Any resemblance to actual historical events or people is pure coincidence.

Copyright © 2020 by J. T. Skye

No part of this book may be reproduced in any form or by any electronic or mechanical means, including information storage and retrieval systems, without written permission from the author, except for the use of brief quotations in a book review.

Table of Contents4

Prologue 1 - Tuesday August 1, 1939 6
Prologue 2 - Monday, December 8, 1941 10
Chapter 1 - Trying to escape 12
Chapter 2 - To Find A Plane 18
Chapter 3 - New Beginnings 29
Chapter 4 - Desperate Times 37
Chapter 5 - Returning Home 41
Chapter 6 - Heading South 52
Chapter 7 - Out With The Old 57
Chapter 8 - A Meeting 60
Chapter 9 - The Ravine 65
Chapter 10 - An Evaluation And A Revelation 74
Chapter 11 - Independence 81
Chapter 12 - Discovery 88
Chapter 13 - Enlightenment 95
Chapter 14 - Desperate Times 101
Chapter 15 - An Opportunity Appears 104
Chapter 16 - Success 109
Chapter 17 - The First Recovery 115
Chapter 18 - A Fatal Setback 126
Chapter 19 - The Second Recovery 132
Chapter 20 - A Surprise Awaits 137
Chapter 21 - A Dire Turn 140

Chapter 22 - Revelation...145

Chapter 23 - Girding 150

Chapter 24 - Finding The Bomb..152

Chapter 25 - New Eyes...165

Prologue 1 - Tuesday August 1, 1939

The Japanese Ambassador to the United States sat with perfect posture at the small red and white gingham covered dining table, flanked on both sides by his 3 meticulously dressed, younger, male assistants, standing perfectly straight behind him. They were the only patrons in the New Orleans cafe on this hot and muggy summer day.

The ambassador finished signing the bottom of the short, 2 page, roughly typed treaty with his characteristic small and very precise signature. He was very focused at completing the task with a hint of a smile beginning to form in his otherwise inscrutable face.

He was thinking about the enormous magnitude of the event and the empirical importance of the document.

He ignored the many misspelled words in both Japanese and in German set in faded type on the brilliant white, bond typing paper, conveniently and coincidentally made in the United States of America. His nose wrinkled as he caught the strong whiff of Cajun spices from the near-by kitchen amid the clatter of kitchen staff preparing food for the soon-to-arrive lunch crowd.

He looked up at his German counter part, briefly smiled his thin lipped, enigmatic smile and politely sat back with a short, crisp, gentle nod - his way of saying he was done.

His tall, graying blond, German counterpart, stood several feet away from the small, table, his nervous hands clasped together behind his back, tightly clenched in anticipation of the ambassador signing the treaty and the immense fear if the ambassador had declined to sign and the enormous failure that would represent to his personal well-being.

He gently clicked his boot heels and nodded a short crisp acknowledgment, smiling broadly. Neither one spoke the other's language, but both spoke a small amount of American English and understood each other very well, concluding the 5th and final visit to craft their mutually beneficial Long 90 Accord, as they had now come to refer to the treaty.

    The Japanese Ambassador carefully reviewed the signed copy reflecting light from the small, restaurant chandelier to make sure the ink was completely dry. His assistant quickly stepped forward with a small, white cotton handkerchief to gently dab the now dry signature. He confirmed it was dry. The Japanese Ambassador lifted the treaty and handed it to the German ambassador, his dark suit with crisp, white starched shirt and thin black tie caused him to sweat in the hot, humid New Orleans summer, this August of 1939.

    The Japanese ambassador then quickly re-scanned his signed copy of the treaty labeled the Long 90 Treaty written in German and Japanese. The completion of this momentous agreement was paramount for their quest of western domination, control of key oil and mineral resources Japan desperately needed, and recognized the sovereignty, at least for the *moment*, of each of their empires.

    It was not coincidental but entirely intentional that they met at Longitude 90 degrees West and Latitude 30 degrees North in the American city of New Orleans, Louisiana. That was now the dividing line between the two half worlds, West of that longitude now claimed by Japan and East of that now claimed by Germany.

    They each carefully secured their copy of the treaty in leather bound folders and quickly departed amid the cacophony of ever-present American partying in the French quarter of the bustling city.

    They each went their separate ways, the Japanese traveling by road and sedan to the local airport to board a diplomatic plane back to Tokyo and the Germans to board a large luxury yacht bound for Berlin, each pleased that they had divided the world to their liking with America and the Americans completely oblivious to the treaty signing event.

Prologue 2 - Monday, December 8, 1941

President Franklin Delano Roosevelt waited impatiently until his private secretary, Louis McHenry Howe, quietly closed the Oval Office door behind him as he exited. The President then reached deep into the back of the top, right side drawer to pull out his most HATED document. He scowled with tight lipped anger, his eyes fierce and bright with intense focus, resentment and hatred.

He carefully pulled the 2 page document out of the cardboard folder sleeve and reread it to ensure it was the correct and complete treaty, and that neither of the pages were missing. This was not the time to let either of these pages become public knowledge, now or ever.

Both of the ivory colored pages were there, detailing the American and British agreement with Adolph Hitler to ensure their safe protection from German aggression and attack by granting exclusive agreement that Germany would own all of Europe and Western Russia.

His lips were pressed tightly together in anger, emotion and defiance as he reread the cursed, one page treaty, signed just a year ago, with a second page of hastily scrawled notes of their conversations. His eyes were bright and intense. It had been weighing on him desperately even before the ink was dry that he was feeling forced to sign the convention to protect his precious America and his keen partner Great Britain at such a horrible, horrible cost.

And now it was all for naught.

He reached for the metal waste basket under his desk and the American made Zippo lighter on top. He spun the round striker twice igniting the flame that began to curl around the bottom corner of the dangerous, deadly and controversial agreement. He watched it burn and flare up toward his fingers, then dropped it into the metal basket next to his wheel chair.

He looked at the very brief note on his desk from his top aide - "Germany has attacked England". That event clearly contravened the hastily signed accord, now fully consumed in a pile of ash in the waste basket.

It no longer mattered that he had made an evil treaty with the devil. America was going to war with Germany anyway.

Chapter 1 - Trying to escape

Isabella Elena Torres hacked convulsively, coughing, again and again. Her blood and phlegm sprayed across her cockpit instrument panel. She barely noticed and grimaced as she painfully wheezed to breath in one more time. She was already light-headed from the loss of blood and difficulty breathing.

She fought hard to control the small, 1936 Ercoupe, single engine airplane with the twin rudders. The badly vibrating Continental 40 hp engine was off balance and shaking badly because of the bent tip of the propeller - bent after it struck and killed the German officer. She was pleased the horrible Generalmajor was dead and she had killed him with her plane. She started to smile thinly then started to hack again, spewing more blood across the instrument panel.

But, at least she was able to take off and escape, now heading North toward Caracas and home.

How long she could continue to fly was another question.

She grimaced, again, at the pain from the bullet lodged in the left side of her chest and quickly surveyed the cabin interior with her blood splattered all over the inside of the once immaculate plane. She was jittery and hurting, her blood loss continued draining her life away. She could see her blood pooling in the bottom of the airplane through the bright, full moon light above, shining brightly through the round windshield and canopy. She could feel herself becoming more light headed and groggy as she glanced up.

The sky was so bright, even at midnight because the moon was so full in the cloudless sky, it was so…

No, no…! Time to focus, not admire the night sky. She glanced at her altimeter and her attitude indicator gauge to make sure she was still flying level and then checked her compass to make sure she was heading home.

The sound of the gun shot still rang in her ears - not the shot that cored her, but the shot before… the shot she was sure ended her father's life, Dr. Luis Alberto Torres, Special Envoy to the United States. Tears welled in her eyes again and she fought back, blinking rapidly several times to focus on keeping the small plane level in the sky and flying home. She had to get home, that was his final request of her. Fly home and take the oilskin wrapped documents and box with her. Protect them at any cost. Hide them away and make sure the Germans never get them.

She grimaced at the pain both physical and emotional, the trail of tears still moist at the edges of her eyes. Her normally full lips were now a tight thin line in anger, pain and now fear. Her eyes, dark, clear and fighting the enormous pain. Her nose filled with the smell of her own blood across the interior of the cockpit and the petroleum smell of the wrapped, oil skin covered documents.

The pain was excruciating now, her breathing ever harder and more difficult. She knew she would never make it home, but she knew she had to get away, far, far away so the German family could never get the documents and wooden box her father consigned to her to take away to the family estate.

She glanced down in the passenger seat foot well of the small plane and saw the three rolled and tied, oilskin wrapped documents laying next to the locked wooden box, 30 centimeters by 30 centimeters by 20 centimeters tall. She did not know what any of it was, just that her father had entrusted it to her and hastily commanded… no, BEGGED that she fly her little plane and take the documents North to their estate near Caracas. For just a moment, she was surprised by his request, he never begged, never pleaded and certainly did not like her flying her little airplane. He did not like her flying at all, but now he needed her to fly home. For that tiny moment, she had been pleased.

She again looked out over the vast ocean of undulating jungle, a black, dense carpet in the night. There were no airports, no runways, no roads, just the vast sea of dark jungle in the bright night.

She coughed convulsively again with a deep wheeze. She was so dizzy she could hardly see out of the canopy across the vast landscape below.

In the distance in front of her she saw a brief reflection, a lighter patch in the jungle canopy. She knew she was dying, she knew she'd never make it home. The pain was too great, the blood loss too much and the grogginess getting worse by the moment. Her feet and hands felt cold and numb. She glanced again at the instruments and realized she was not flying level and gently shifted the control wheel to the right to level her flight. She needed a way to land the plane in the night with no lights around her. She forced herself to concentrate through her mental fog to aim her plane for the distant patch. Even this far away she could see in the moon light it was a large, wide grassy area, covered in a shorter bush or grass from the surrounding jungle of trees.

That would have to do. She was fully spent and had no more life to give.

She set her tight lips in a grimace, focused what was left of her waning concentration and aimed the small plane for the field moving the throttle, slowing the airplane down.

She approached the small, grassy field and suddenly remembered to watch her speed gauge.

She hadn't been paying attention and the plane slowed too much, now close to the 77 Kilometers per hour stall speed and weaving, bobbing in the still night air like a drunken sailor.

She concentrated on the speed and horizon indicator, picked a spot near the front edge of the light, grassy patch and aimed for it. The plane continued to wobble as she swiftly approached.

The ground rushed up and smacked the bottom of the small plane with a hard bounce and crunch. The little airplane collapsed to the rough grass covered field, flattening the tricycle style landing gear and skidding forward, swiftly slowing down. She looked around wildly knowing she no longer controlled the craft and was just a passenger now on a bumpy, chaotic ride. The plane's momentum continued to carry it forward and continued to slow down as it approached the end of the grassy field.

Her consciousness was ebbing away with every drop of blood that seeped from her fatal chest wound, then suddenly realized what was in front of her.

Looking straight out, the view crystallized in her mind as she realized the dark, wide patch crossing in front of her wasn't the jungle forest, but a narrow ravine of some kind. She knew her time to die was at hand and embraced her existence, only having a moment of terror as she realized she had not fulfilled her father's dying wish that she fly to the family compound.

Isabella Elena Lopez had a moment of calm acceptance when just before she passed away she saw the edge of the abyss looming up, the plane slowed impossibly at the edge, wobbling, teetering, seeming to come to a rest, pausing for a moment as it finally stopped… and then she and her broken plane gently slid over and into the narrow chasm below. With her last breath she mouthed an apology to her father and finally, forever lost consciousness as the plane tipped over the edge, falling toward the rushing rapids and boulders below.

She and the tiny plane never made it to the bottom, never made it to the torrential rapids and waterfalls below.

Chapter 2 - To Find A Plane

Morgan finished the short argument with his wife, Melissa, on his satellite phone - "I'm sorry honey, I told you we'll be home in a couple of days, I promise. Yes, I know I said I wouldn't do these anymore, but this one is safe. Give me a break here, I'm just trying to pay the bills, honey." He grimaced with thin-lipped sadness, paused as she responded, then he added with a bit of frustration and sarcasm, "This is Canada, dear, not the Middle East…" He barely said that as she angrily hung up her side of the conversation.

He looked up at the deep blue Yukon, Canadian sky for a moment, closed his eyes to concentrate and let go of the frustration, anger and disappointment he felt. He loved her so much, but she was so angry that he still did this aircraft salvage work. He had promised her he wouldn't do these anymore, but this one was safe. It wasn't like before and he needed to do something to pay the bills - his heavy lift construction company just didn't have enough contracts at the moment to make ends meet. He was filled with frustration and disappointment at his inability to provide for his wife, to provide for their life. It was all just so unfair and now he'd really angered her.

He stared back down for a moment at the small satellite phone with disappointment and sadness. The premature aging lines in his deeply tanned face emphasized his tight lipped grimace and told the whole story. She was tired of his adventures, tired of his being away, tired of their money troubles. She was just plain tired and he didn't blame her.

He put the satellite phone in the small pocket of his day-pack, pulled off his bright, sky-blue cap and rubbed his short, prematurely gray, hair back. His powerfully muscled arms and shoulders stretched the long sleeve, red and white cotton shirt inside his tight fitting down vest. He took a deep breath to calm and clear his mind. He still had a job to do.

He looked up at the brilliant, cloudless, deep cobalt blue sky, trying to take the stress out of his neck and shoulders, wishing he could provide a better life for her and for them. He loved her so much. He wished deeply she would try to understand his immense fear of not providing, his need to feel confident he was contributing. She was his bedrock, she had kept him together after he came home from Iraqi Freedom and his tours in Afghanistan.

He cocked his neck from side to side and heard it click, crack and crunch as his taught, powerful neck muscles stretched.

His distracted focus came back when he looked out at the bright, dry, craggy expanse of Canadian wilderness with the large, enormously vertical patches of Northern Pine chunked in broad expanses, like large, dark green, vertical islands. The air smelled strongly of the pine and a special sharpness he often found in the high mountains. He never got tired of that smell.

He had stopped at this spot and was intentionally standing at the edge of one of the tree islands that dotted the broad, rocky landscape. He had picked this spot out specifically. Now, he needed to finish the deal, so they could go home.

His friend and mentor Tony Fisher stood a discrete distance away, carefully inspecting his already bitten-down fingernails and then surveyed the broad, gray and brown rough, rock fields that undulated below them into the distance.

Tony turned away to look at the swiftly approaching, clearly angry field supervisor, arms and legs pumping strongly up and down like pistons as he huffed his red-faced and very over-weight body up the rocky hill toward the two of them. He clearly was not happy.

Morgan said, "It seems like we never get a break."

Tony responded, "I heard a quote once that sometimes you gotta make your own break."

Morgan, "How?"

Tony looked at him, "That's what you have to figure out. That is what makes you special and why you have this strange gift of finding and salvaging planes."

Tony looked at the approaching figure with a deep focus and spoke just loudly enough for Morgan to hear. "You know you gotta do right by her Morgan."

"I know, I know, but as hard as I try, it feels like she just doesn't understand me. Ever since I got back. She's changed. She should support the work I do."

"Hey man, did you ever think that maybe you are the one that changed? What you experienced in the war would change anyone. You gotta know that, right? And, maybe you need a bit less attitude about it."

He watched the clearly angry field supervisor painfully drag his very overweight body up the rocky slope toward them.

"We gotta finish this, find the plane so we can salvage it and you can pay your debts." Tony paused for just a moment and then added gently, "Maybe buying the helicopter wasn't as smart as you thought."

"Yeah, I know it, now we argue all the time about money and the bills."

"I understand, but maybe buying the Skycrane wasn't the smartest thing to do since it costs so much to keep it."

"Well, maybe… but I really think I can make it pay for itself hauling logs, or large air-conditioners or dropping water for fire control. I got such a great deal on it. I just have to show her I can do it. That's the ticket."

They both paused to look at the swiftly approaching field project supervisor clearly so angry he was talking to himself, angrily and waving his hands back and forth, frothing spit hanging on the edge of his lower lip.

"So, Morgan," Tony looked ominous, trying to give Morgan his best serious expression, "The MAN is approaching, and I'm really thinking now that he doesn't look too happy. I'm not sure what you are seeing with him, but I'm just not sure he's feeling the love right now, if you know what I mean. "

Tony paused for a moment, then added, "Sooooo... what are we going to tell him?"

Morgan turned to his close friend and smiled broadly, confidently as he looked at Tony, then the approaching figure and changed to a serious expression, "The truth of course. Always the truth, you know that Tony. Yes, I have attitude, but it will always be the truth."

Tony chuckled, looked at the ground and shook his head wearily. "I know you have this weird way of finding these things, but even this one has been a bitch. You have got to admit that. Right? Do you have any idea where this thing is? The man is here and I 'kinda think he's going to want some answers. He looks a bit pissy if you know what I mean."

Morgan flashed a smile for a millisecond, winked quickly at Tony, then just nodded twice as Nathan Brandstad stopped up short of them, clearly angry, huffing, red faced and out of breath at the high altitude, near tree-line stretch of remote Northern Canadian wilderness they were standing in.

He paused for a moment to catch his breath, coughed up phlegm from his lungs spitting it out on the hard scrabble, then started in, red faced from the hike and the sunburn, clearly worked up now and flat-out mad.

"When the fuck are you boys goin' to join this search to find this plane! You are supposed to be these hot-shot salvage experts and haven't produced SHIT." He paused to breathe, rasping air filled his lungs and then spread his arms out toward the rest of the project crew, diligently searching for small airplane bits over and under rocks and boulders out across the rocky landscape.

He continued loudly, "We're all up here doin' the team thing to try and work together to find where it crashed. Clearly, you aren't participating in that. You are supposed to be so good at this, where is the damn plane?"

Morgan pressed his lips into a thin tight line focused intently on Nathan, then, smiled thinly, playing with him, badly baiting him, "A plane will only be found when it wants to."

Tony just closed his eyes for a moment, shaking his head with mild despair, knowing that was like throwing gas on the fire. He started to interrupt the tirade, "Mr. Brandstad..."

Nathan just waived his hand to shut him up. "We've been up here for two fucking days and haven't found a scrap of wreckage, not one fucking scrap! You keep telling me it is here, but we haven't found so much as a paper clip. Well, Mr. HOT SHOT expert, where the hell is it? You only make salvage money if we find the plane."

He paused again to suck in more air, "What? Is this like some kind of vacation for you two? YOU'VE wasted all of the project funds, for what - a fun trip in the Canadian wilderness - the HIGH fucking altitude, Canadian wilderness? I can't believe we are doing this. Where the hell is the plane? You two are such losers. LOSERS!"

Morgan started to speak but was cut off with a waive of his hand.

He looked sternly at Morgan and then at Tony then swept his hand out to the broad expanse of the field. "Look out there at our team, CAREFULLY canvassing the grid, ONE section at a time, looking carefully at and under each rock just to make sure we've got the field covered. That's how things get done. That's how planes get found… you find bits and pieces, then you find more pieces and then you get to find the plane. You guys are up here taking a fucking break while the TEAM down there is doin' all the WORK. Does any part of that sound wrong to you? Are you guys getting it yet? We need to find that plane or you won't get a dime of salvage money."

Morgan waited for Brandstad to pause for air, focused on Nathan, grimaced again and looked vastly disappointed, turned to look at Tony then back to Nathan. "We won't make any money on this salvage at all, Mr. Brandstad. Do you see any large junks of plane out there where the team is? No, right? We might as well leave now."

Nathan expelled more phlegm then added quickly, "Exactly, if you can't find the damn plane, you can't salvage it. What a fuckin' waste of time you are!"

Morgan shook his head in disagreement, turned fully and started cracking the knuckles of his left hand, "Mr. Brandstad, I don't agree and you misunderstand me. Our deal was you pay us $5 grand each to find it and $50 grand to salvage it if you couldn't get to it, right?"

"Yeah, but unless I need glasses," he yelled shaking his head, waving his hands, "I don't see any fucking airplane."

"Exactly, that is the problem you don't seem to understand."

Morgan shifted his weight, then motioned with his hand and fingers for them to follow him, then slowly walked about 10 feet over toward the trunk of one of the big Northern Pines at the edge of the forested stand of pine. He looked at Brandstad, then pointed down at the ground. "'See that?"

Nathan couldn't see anything so he slowly, now painfully and angrily stepped over, still tired from the ordeal of hiking up the slope to meet them, still becoming angrier by the moment.

On the ground were several dark drops of an amber colored liquid. "What, you have me looking at tree sap now?" he shared dramatically, his spit rocketing out of the side of his mouth, "We're supposed to be looking for an airplane, you know, those things that fly in the air! You are such a fucking loser… both of you!"

Morgan sat down on his haunches, smiled broadly and gently touched the thin, amber liquid, picking some up with his right index finger, rolling it between the pads of his thumb and index finger. He looked up at them then easily, lithely stood up and strode over to Tony and Nathan, with a confident, knowing look, "So, you don't know what this is, then? Because THIS is the key."

Brandstad paused momentarily confused, then returned with his sarcastic anger, "No, what is it?"

Morgan looked at Tony then back at Nathan.

Tony smiling broadly from ear to ear, exclaimed loudly, "Oh, Morgan – my heavens but you are good. You are very, very good! Engine oil? Really? Morgan, you continue to amaze me even after all of these years doing this work. Wow, you are good."

Brandstad interrupted loudly, "No way! If that is engine oil, where's the damn plane?" He turned slowly as he swept his hand around to the broad expanse of the rocky land in front of them, "Do you see it here, do you SEE any airplane? Do you see any pieces? Parts? A CRASH site? You both are losing it, you tell me you're some hot shot salvage guy and you show me a drip of oil, then WHERE the hell is the airplane?"

Morgan smiled broadly and simply added, "Exactly Mr. Brandstad. It is a drip. And you are right, we aren't going to make a dime on this salvage, because you won't need us to extricate the plane for you, you can do it all by yourself."

Morgan was smiling and clearly baiting Nathan. Nathan took it hook, line and sinker, "Where? Where is it? I don't see any plane, where the HELL is it?" he shouted both arms floundering around in frustration, confusion and anger.

Morgan smiled, looked him straight in the eyes and simply pointed up into the tall expanse of the tree. "It's up there. You can send the $5 thousand you owe us for finding it and pull the airplane down on your own. You've got the TEAM here to do it. You don't need us to do that job. That was the deal. Right? We are done here."

He motioned to Tony and they both walked away, Morgan calmly looking down the rock path and Tony still smiling from ear to ear, gently shaking his head in amazement.

Nathan stopped for a moment in surprise as they began to walk away, then craned his neck back. He stumbled on the rocks as he backed away from the tree stand to look up as high as he could see and just saw the glint of sunlight on the white rudder more than a hundred feet up. The plane had crashed alright, just not on the ground. It had crashed into the side of the tree and stuck there, the cracked engine crankcase leaking oil onto the hard, rocky ground below.

Morgan and Tony just walked away, carefully stepping through the loose scree down the slope back toward their rented Jeep and home.

Chapter 3 - New Beginnings

Generalmajor Johan Schmid bristled at the delay with thin lipped anger, arrogance and resentment. He and his family were not used to traveling in a freight truck. He was used to riding in the back of a Mercedes Benz staff car, chauffeured every where he went by his assigned driver. But they needed to get to the port and this was the fastest way with their special cargo.

His hand and arm were extended out to the dashboard as if to push the truck further, faster. His driver looked briefly sideways with concern. "We will make the boat heir Generalmajor." He then pushed the center button of the steering wheel and the anemic horn blurted out their anger at the stalled truck traffic in front of them.

The driver eased up on the long clutch to inch further forward and continued to steer the small freight truck further on.

An eternal hour later, they arrived at the port and pulled up in front of a German fishing trawler with its small pole crane poised over the dock. He surveyed the small, 30 meter long boat with a mixture of anger, dread, fear, disappointment, growing realization, resignation… mixed with a bit of odd happiness.

He stepped out of the cab, went to the back, opened the flap and helped his wife carefully step down from the tail gate, then his 3 children. His adjutant and brother Karl, and his wife also jumped down. Together they were making a break for a new life, a new land in a new world. Karl Schmid handed him a short, curt telegram he had received before they had hastily loaded onto the truck to escape the American and Russian forces sweeping through the city. He looked briefly at the note that advised his package had arrived in the New World as planned. He nodded, smiling and pointed at the Captain of the fishing boat to pull out the remaining freight. The dock crew quickly pulled off the back of the truck canvas and attached the heavy duty tow cable to the small-car sized freight box in the bed of the truck. As the crane began to lift away, the boat tilted toward the truck until the heavy crate slowly lifted free. The Captain vigorously shouted and motioned for his crew to move it over the top of the boat and settle it down on the deck.

Generalmajor Schmid yelled, "Carefully heir Kapitan… it is… is delicate inside."

The Captain angrily waved his hand and walked over to directly face Schmid with his hand out. Schmid smiled broadly and nodded crisply, every man has his price, reached into his inside tunic and pulled out an thick envelope.

The Captain opened it and carefully counted the unbelievable sum of $1000 American dollars in $20 dollar bills. He carefully scanned all 50 of the bills and shoved it inside his inside jacket pocket, then zipped the front closed. He nodded to Schmid then motioned for the Generalmajor and family to board the boat by walking up the 1 meter wide, wooden board on the side of the dock.

The adjutant's wife boarded as well and the adjutant supervised the loading of the rest of their personal luggage and boxes. A short hour later, the truck had vanished back into traffic and the trawler was beginning to chug slowly away from the Hamburg pier and down the River Elbe, toward the North Sea.

Generalmajor Schmid stood at the back of the boat looking out as Germany passed away behind them. He was profoundly disappointed in her obvious defeat, but knew that he had to move his families away or face the judgment court for his ethnic cleansing on behalf of the Fatherland. He had excelled at his ability to round up and rid the Fatherland of the hated Jewish presence. Only with it gone could the Fatherland have grown into its new ideal. But the Jews from other countries would not, could not let that happen and the Fatherland was now being overrun by the Americans and Russians doing the evil Jewish bidding.

He was pleased that they had escaped and that they would now make a new life in South America. He chuckled, the Americans were actively searching for him, hunting for him even now, and he'd escape to their Southern name sake.

He walked around to the main deck and looked at the wooden freight box that had almost caused the boat to tilt. He knew what was in it and the enormous, devastatingly lethal power it contained. He knew it was very experimental, but the Jewish scientist vowed it would work and it would be the largest explosion in history. He understood a tiny amount of the science and math involved, but believed the Jewish scientist… just before he executed him. The scientist had referred to it as the AtomeBombe. A bomb made from special atoms that could instantly devastate an entire city. That was just one of the many treasures he had stolen to ensure his safe travel, comfort and wealth in the new world.

Three days later with his wife and children still green, dizzy and seasick they transferred the big case to the special submarine he had sent orders to meet them. The submersible boat was special and unique in the German navy because it had a freight hatch large enough to take the small, car sized nuclear weapon and their boxes of personal belongings.

When the sub was sealed and moving away, he motioned to the Captain and pulled him aside from his crew. "The Kapitan of the fishing trawler is not one of us. He made comments about how he likes to tell stories of his adventures and shared he was from Poland and a family of wealthy merchants. I am concerned he will not… not take our oath seriously. Kapitan, he may divulge where we are taking this secret shipment and the path your are sailing. His boat needs to be destroyed so he cannot talk."

The Captain focused on the Generalmajor, nodded in disappointment of the news a fellow seaman would and could be treasonous. He turned and gave the order for his crew to begin to move the submarine away from the fishing trawler.

As they pulled away, he gave the order for the single aft torpedo tube door to be opened and to be filled with water. When that was completed, he signaled for the launch of the torpedo. The TV G7es 5.35 meter long Zaunkonig torpedo left the tube and accelerated to full speed hitting the center mass of the fishing trawler just below the water line and exploding in a bright flash. Generalmajor Schmid turned to the Captain, looked him in the eyes, with fierce determination and nodded grimly, "For the Fatherland." The Captain simply nodded back, then turned to guide the submarine away.

The rest of the trip to Caracas Venezuela was uneventful other than the family slowly becoming less seasick. The Captain ran on the surface most of the time, submerging only when close to Atlantic sea lanes or when they spotted distant ships. Their goal, their mission, was to get the Generalmajor, his family and top secret cargo away from Germany and safely, secretly to the new world where the Fatherland could start anew.

Generalmajor Schmidt firmly believed the Fatherland was betrayed from inside by sympathizers and from the Jewish plague, but he was more pragmatic than that. Regardless of the success of the German high command in this new world, he wanted his family to live in luxury and comfort. He and they had grown accustomed to that life. He would work to continue that lifestyle.

Stealing, the bomb, the secret treaty, the geographic mineral maps, the Jewish jewelry and the large amount of cash was intended to secure their long term comfort and wealth. The Fatherland had failed and now he would take matters into his own hand, secure their future and start anew.

When they arrived in Caracas, his second adjutant met them at the dock with two cars and a small cargo truck. The big German U Boat was the only one in the harbor and was instantly a big attraction.

Generalmajor Schmid climbed out of the front to join the sub's crew finishing the unloading of the family and possessions. Schmid turned to the Captain,

"Thank you heir Kapitan. You have been a fine friend and patriot of the Fatherland. You are helping us start over and we all appreciate that."

He clapped his hand on the Captain's shoulder as a sign of comradeship to ask what his next mission was.

"I go hunting for war ships as before and then back to Germany." Schmid nodded and wished him good hunting for the Fatherland then walked briskly down the ramp.

Schmid's road car followed by his brother Karl's car slowly wound up the hill toward their new, temporary estate. He glanced out at the distant horizon and checked his watch, watching the second hand click toward the top of the hour. He instructed the driver to stop, motioning him to pull over on the side of the road, near the edge of the cliff and continued to watch. The minute hand hit the top of the hour and he glanced up, expectantly. In the far distance he could see a sudden puff of smoke and flame as the satchel bomb he had planted in the torpedo room detonated. He looked calmly out at the growing, billowing smoke and shared in a whisper, "For our future freedom and NOT… the Fatherland."

Generalmajor Schmid motioned for the driver to continue on to their new home and turned away from the vestiges of his horrific past as it sank into the sea behind them.

Chapter 4 - Desperate Times

Dr. Luis Alberto Torres, special envoy to the United States of America burst into the small library where his daughter sat reading a romantic novel. She immediately glanced up in surprise and closed the book with her finger on the page she'd been reading. Her dear father never did anything fast or spontaneous. He was always, thoughtful, methodical and precise. He quickly surveyed the room and rushed over to close the thick curtains to block the inside light from seeping into the evening outside.

He rushed over to his small safe under his desk, "My dearest Isabella, I know I have often been critical of your passion for flying that dreaded little airplane, but I must ask you to fly it now, tonight, immediately.

"What is it father, what is wrong?"

"That Generalmajor will arrive shortly and he must not find you here!" Luis finally cranked open the short, floor safe and extracted three oil skin pouches and a latched wooden box. He quickly stood and rushed over to her. "Please my dear, you must hurry." He said as she laid the book on the side table and quickly stood up. He handed the pouches and box to Isabella. "Please you must hurry and take these now to our home in the North. Leave right now… please leave right now. Can you do that, will the plane fly at night?"

"Yes father I can fly at night as long as the moon is full and there are no storms. What is wrong what is happening."

He grabbed her arm and led her forcefully to the library door, "Please go right now. I can't let the Generalmajor find these here. Take them and run. Take them to our home and hide them."

She quickly grabbed her thin jacket and ran out the door to the small motor scooter at the side of their small home. She quickly started and zoomed off. In her mirror, she could see the swiftly approaching headlamps of several cars so she twisted the throttle as far as it would go. The small scooter jumped and bounced ahead taking her the short distance to the small airfield the local natives had hacked out of the jungle wilderness.

Her 1939 Ercoupe twin tailed airplane sat at the end of the runway just as she'd left it. The tank would be full as she always filled it after each flight. She ducked in front and pulled the short wooden chock blocks from the front wheel she used to prevent it from moving in the occasional wind.

She stepped up on the plane and quickly set the box and oilskins in the passenger seat. Settling into the left seat she pulled the short choke knob out about a centimeter, looked quickly around. It was then she heard the single gun shot back at her father's home. She worriedly glanced back through the large jungle trees to see if she could see anything there. Her view was blocked so she quickly turned off the magneto and turned the small 40 hp Continental, horizontally opposed piston engine. It cranked over smoothly.

She looked back toward the house again and could see the flickering movement of cars on the road. That could only mean they were coming for her.

She switched the magnetos on and cranked the engine starter again. This time it coughed, gently then smoothly started up. She clipped her seat belt and harness and moved the throttle forward to begin to roll the small twin tailed airplane forward.

She looked over and saw the cars swiftly approaching the small runway. She accelerated the small plane and it bumped up and over the short edge of the cut grass strip.

A swiftly approaching car stopped a short distance and several men jumped from the vehicle before it was fully stopped and ran toward her plane from midway down the runway. Vowing not to get stopped, she pushed the plane forward applying the full throttle and simultaneously pushing down the flaps to prepare for a quick take off. Only then did she turn on the navigation lights shining brightly at the running men.

Generalmajor Schmid was in front, running as fast as he could his arms pumping like pistons with a Luger pistol in his left hand.

The little Ercoupe was picking up speed but would not be able to take off before the men reached her. She pushed the airplane's control wheel a bit forward and to the left causing the accelerating plane to veer toward the men. He saw the change in her lights and realized she was swiftly approaching and aiming at them. He stopped short, fully out of breath, took careful aim and pulled the trigger. His first shot went wild and behind the plane. He quickly re-aimed the weapon, paused his breath and fired again more accurately as her plane was on them. The swiftly spinning propeller sliced his left arm and chest into many strips, killing him and bending the thin metal tip of the aluminum propeller.

The other 3 men instantly dove out of the way of the plane. They rolled on the ground, stopped themselves, spun around with hand guns drawn, but the small plane was already airborne and wobbly, chaotically, lifting away over the tree tops. They rushed back to the Generalmajor but he was already dead. The plane, girl and secret contents he had so desperately tried to capture had escaped.

Chapter 5 - Returning Home

Morgan walked into his log home and knew it was empty. He could feel it. There was no life in it. Melissa wasn't there. He could feel it, feel her presence when he walked into their home. There was a special feeling when he walked into the home before and he could sense her presence there. It wasn't any special sensory perception, just... well, he had these feelings, like he could smell her essence or hear small sounds. Now there were none. Tony thought he had a gift, but he could just, well, sense when she was near by.

And, the lights were all off. Yeah, that was likely it.

He walked through the hall to the kitchen and looked out the panoramic windows out at the back and the big, flowing vistas beyond. That is why they'd bought this mountain home, for the vistas.

He could just see the source of her current frustration off to the side of the window, the tail rotor of his Sikorsky Skycrane, the enormous helicopter he'd purchased at a steep discount when his friend's dad liquidated the small construction company after being indicted for money laundering, embezzlement and fraud. He thought it was such a great deal and that it would make them financially secure. Boy, was he wrong.

He just stared out, sadness filling him with a wetness filling his eyes. She'd worked so hard to pull him out of the abyss of the war, worked so hard to help them as a couple and now she was gone. He felt so alone and so uncertain. His lifeline to his world had said goodbye.

Morgan dropped his small duffel bag on the deep burgundy stained, oak floors and reached for the note on top of the stack of bills on the kitchen island. He turned it around to read her crisp, flowing calligraphic style, "I can't take it anymore. You have to figure your life out on your own now."

His eyes welled up and he blinked several times to try and stop the tears. Melissa wasn't one to mince words and she didn't play false cards. What she said, she did. He took a deep breath in and sat down in one of the lounge chairs. She'd most likely go and stay with her mother, 79 and still strong as a whip.

Morgan looked up and around at the interior, the broad, tall, cathedral ceiling and the wide wooden, carpet covered steps leading up to their bedroom. He loved this house, this home, but now it seemed so empty. He just looked out, unsure of how to fix this, how to win her back, how to pay all of their, no, how to pay all of HIS bills.

He quickly scanned the open bills and statements. He briefly shook his head in disappointment and sadness. His construction company bank account had $12.73 available and the first bill in the stack was for his $2,755 helicopter fuel bill. The second bill was for the insurance for the helicopter and airplane. The third bill was a notice that an annual inspection was due on the big Sikorsky 'copter. He was so over his head. He'd have to give up the helicopter and the plane to even try and save the house. She deserved her half.

She had the head for business, he didn't, she had the focus and drive to make the phone calls and ask for payments, he didn't. He was the doer. He could fly anything, anywhere, any way, any time, in any conditions. But that needed a partnership and he'd blown that buying the big helicopter and the small Kitfox, high wing, 2 place airplane. Well, they'd talked about the need to sell them and now he'd have to figure out how to do just that. He couldn't procrastinate any more or the bank would take the house too. What a mess he'd created and realized he had no clue of how to fix it.

For the first time in his life, Morgan began to feel… 'desperate'.

He just settled back looking up at the ceiling and then out across the forested vistas and valley beyond the window. In another life, he would have opened a bottle of single malt scotch to drown his troubles, but she'd taught him that just made the morning worse, 'cause the troubles were still there in the morning and you'd need a ton of aspirin to cure the headache.

The afternoon sun was setting and beginning to fill the huge expanse of glass. He got out of the sunken seat and walked out on the deck to open the BBQ. Morgan put some paper in the bottom of his small, steel chimney and natural hickory charcoal in the top, then lit the paper to get the coals going. He walked back in and opened the refrigerator to take out a steak but there weren't any, not un-frozen, anyway. He shook his head in disappointment, one more thing she did that he missed. She always was thinking ahead.

He reached into the freezer to take out a steak and put it in the fridge to thaw for tomorrow. The vegetables were gone, meat gone, 'nothing perishable was left.

Then it struck him. She still thought he would be salvaging an airplane and wouldn't be home for several weeks at least. Always thinking ahead, she was always thinking ahead. He looked up and outside. It was too late to stop the BBQ, so he just let the charcoal burn in the chimney. There was no wind this evening and the BBQ was protected in its corner. Besides, it was still wet from the late snows and rain, so he didn't have to worry about fire.

He processed that as he walked into the their pantry, no… now his pantry and pulled out a can of chili for dinner. He found a half bottle of Baco Noir from Southern Oregon and poured a half glass of that with the chili.

He felt exhausted and tired from the ordeal in Canada. They'd at least talked the supervisor out of a small finder's fee, so he and Tony both had $5,000 from the trip, but that was hardly a dent in his bills, now and half of that would go to Melissa anyway. Yes, he thought, he'd play this straight. This wasn't about being petty, he'd brought this on himself with the "toys" so he'd play it straight with her. He'd deposit the check and send her half. That was the least he could do and he was terrific at doing the least he could do. That would have to change. He'd need to figure out how to make his life work now. He had no choice but to figure it out. And maybe save his marriage and win back the love of his life.

Morgan quietly ate dinner and slowly sipped his half glass of wine on the expansive back deck, enjoying the setting sun, gentle, whispering breath of wind and the rich pine smell of the woods and forests around him. He looked off to his right at the big Skycrane.

He could see the concrete pad it sat on and the enormous 65 foot diameter rotor. It really did look like a praying mantis from the back.

He just called it the Mule. That was his very un-creative name for it because it just seemed like the right name, it was like a pack animal to him. It could carry enormous weights effortlessly with the two huge gas turbine engines perched on top behind the small 3 person cabin, looking more like a set of huge insect eyes instead of his "office", the place he worked from when hauling heavy loads.

That was his gift, well one of them anyway. He and the Mule were one, they communicated to each other in a way he couldn't do with any other helicopter. It had a feel he could understand and he was very good at flying it.

The only other gift he had is that he could occasionally divine where wrecks were. Well, Tony thought so anyway and that was important. When they were in Kabul, he'd worked out where the downed intelligence drone was and figured out how to extract it in the middle of a hot zone.

He'd figured out where a black ops helicopter had crashed and worked with Tony to pull that out too. He didn't do anything special or weird, 'just put the pieces together in his mind until they made sense and then went to check it out. More often than not, his intuition was accurate. Tony had recognized that very early on and worked with him, cajoled him, joked with him and pushed him to listen to it. Maybe he had some kind of gift, maybe not, but it certainly didn't help him get construction work and pay the bills.

He shook his tired head and looked up at the now fully dark sky. Their home was far enough away from Sacramento and the other large cities that he didn't have a lot of light pollution. He admired the broad expanse of the milky way laying at an angle above him. There was no moon and he could even see a couple of planets, Mars certainly with its clearly reddish hue and maybe Jupiter, too, but really faint. At least the bright light didn't twinkle so maybe it was Jupiter. He really loved coming home here and experiencing the incredible feeling of the mountains, forests, trees and vistas. He was really tired and as he walked through the doors he wondered if he would be able to keep it much longer. That was a mission for tomorrow, to figure out his next steps and to give her the half she deserved.

Morgan slept in late to 6 AM and woke with a start, then looked at his clock. He smiled briefly realizing he'd been really tired if he slept that late, normally getting up around 4:30 by his internal clock.

His mind instantly went to the heavy burden of what to do next and how to sell the Sikorsky and Kitfox to pay his bills and save the house.

He looked out at the windows and the morning was already underway with a light fog sitting flat on the broad valley below. He trotted down the steps to the kitchen, past the big oil landscapes they had worked on together and pulled out a pod to make coffee. He'd clearly been tired as he'd left his small phone on the highly figured cream and mottled brown granite counter. When he tapped the screen, he saw he'd missed a text from Tony. All it said was 'Call me, we have work.' Morgan looked surprised at the text, waited for the coffee to finish and tapped his thumbprint to open the phone. He tapped Tony's number and waited. He answered on the first buzz.

Morgan didn't wait. "Hey Tony, I saw your text. Are you home, did you get home safely?"

"Yeah, I made it home fine. Listen, Morg, I got another job for us and it is pretty urgent. Are you up for it?"

Morgan laughed thinly, "Come on Tony, you know I don't have anything going on. We just got home last night. We barely paid the expenses from the last trip and just got home. What you got?"

There was a long pause and then Tony started in, "I have a chance for you to clear your debt, all of your debt and all legit."

"Yeah, you said that last time."

"No, no, really, I mean it."

"What is it this time?"

"Well…" Tony paused to carefully frame up his next words… "I did some work for a guy once. He's a spook."

"What agency?"

"Don't know but smells a bit like he's CIA."

"How can you tell."

"They all use different words, have different phrases and dress differently. He just kinda feels like CIA to me, 'kinda like the ones we saw in Kabul."

"K, what did you do for him."

"Come on Morg, you know I can't discuss that."

"Okay, what's the job then, what are we doing and why?"

"I can't really tell you that either, other than he needs a plane pulled."

"What can you tell me."

"It means traveling to South America."

"Why."

"A plane went down in Colombia."

"Okay. So, is that rare? Should we like… call the newspapers? Alert CNN?"

"Morg, it went down in 1945 to be precise."

"And we care now why?"

"For two reasons."

"They are?"

"The first is they just found the plane hanging upside down in a tight, shear ravine above a river that no one has yet been able to get down to."

"And number 2?"

"He'll pay us $150K EACH to pull it intact with all of the contents."

"Tony, that's a lot of money for a simple pull, especially when they already know where the plane is. What's the catch, there has to be a catch… there is ALWAYS a catch if they are involved and are paying cash."

"Several teams have tried but no one has figured out how to pull the plane and he is in a rush to get it out. He is desperate so called me."

"Why is this important now after, what, 75 years?"

"I don't know and he wouldn't tell me if I asked."

"Who is the 'he'?"

"His name is George Bolton, or at least that is the name he is using at present. Are you in or out."

"Not sure I have a choice." He signed as he looked at the pile of bills, "I guess for now, I'm in."

"Good. Pack quickly."

"Why? What's going on? Why do I need to pack… quickly?"

"Because they are likely at your front door now with your ticket. I told him you were the guy who could get it done."

He chuckled then smiled broadly at his friend's quick and sometimes odd sense of humor as he tapped the phone to end the call.

Morgan chuckled again for a moment, then stopped when he heard a hard rap on his front door and then the door bell rang.

Chapter 6 - Heading South

Morgan settled into the coach seat, too small for his broad, muscular shoulders and lanky legs. And, too small for Tony with his broad shoulders and growing girth. He tried to give Tony space to tuck his water in the seat pocket in front and to pull up his seat belt to sit down.

The space in these regional airliners was just too small, or too small for he and Tony anyway.

He sniffed for a moment to breath in the slight essence of the Naphtha-Kerosene blended Jet B fuel that wafted in through the open door. It brought back good memories from every time he had flown and been on the tarmac on tour. Most people didn't like the smell of aviation gas, but Morgan did. And it reminded him of his Sikorsky Skycrane, too.

He had won the coin toss and sat next to the window. That meant Tony was the "spread", the stuff in between the two halves of bread that got squished in between.

Tony managed to get his belt wrapped around and clipped together. Morgan waited for him to settle in and scrunched his back and shoulders around toward the window to give Tony a bit more room.

Morgan quietly asked and sarcastically, "Tell me more about the spook."

Tony grimaced for a moment, looked around and shared quietly, "Morgan, they aren't all bad."

"I haven't met any good ones yet, they are all weird, arrogant and conceited."

"They are all highly trained and very competent. Some of that special personality will often leak through even when they are trying to be nice. They aren't all bad people, Morgan. Your attitude about them doesn't help either."

Morgan frowned and sighed in quiet disbelief.

Tony continued, "And you are not above being a bit odd or arrogant yourself sometimes. Like that little show you put on in Canada. You could just have told him, radioed it in or pointed up at the tree, right?"

Morgan paused, letting his friend's words sink in, "I guess so, but he was so ripe for it with his holier-than-thou attitude. So, tell me more about who hired us and what we got ourselves into."

Tony smiled briefly as he looked at Morgan, "He was born to it. He really lives and breathes this stuff, a dedicated lifer."

"Yeah? One of the big gung-ho types?"

"No, this one's a thinker. He's like maybe 5 foot 8, max. And not a lifter, kinda wiry. He thinks his way through stuff, probably mid-fifties, but looks old, like 70s, gray thinning hair, lots of stress wrinkles, you know what I mean. Not mousy but not big either. Lots of mileage and it shows." Tony paused to listen to the Flight Attendant joke about the plane safety in a pleasantly funny, yet informative way.

When the dialog waned, Morgan turned back from the window and added, "And now he needs us to pull out a plane? That's it, just pull it out?"

"Yeah, that sounds way too easy. George is not that generous with taxpayer money. It sounds easy but he wouldn't be calling in the favor unless he was desperate and having problems." He shared sarcastically, then added, "Now that we are on our way, I can share more about his request. It isn't the plane he wants, it's what's in it."

Morgan looked at Tony quizzically, "So, what's in it?"

"He wasn't very, uh… specific, but that is the job. Pull the plane and recover the contents intact. Emphasis on contents first, plane second. At ANY cost. They haven't even been able to get a line or climber down to the plane, its that tough.

"Uh, okay, that sounds like a problem." Morgan furrowed his eye brows, then added with sudden realization, "I'm just not sure what I can offer. It sounds like they already know where the plane is."

"Yeah, like a big problem. And, that is why I wanted you here. You have that uncanny way of finding planes and figuring salvage stuff out. You found that plane in Canada, right under his nose - right under his freaking NOSE!"

"Yeah, but he was a bureaucratic idiot."

"You found those copters and that drone in Afghanistan and Iraq, and pulled them out when everyone else said it couldn't be done… and George KNEW about you. He'd already heard about those gigs."

"Tony, you could do the same, I'm nothing special. Some days I can't tie my shoe laces."

Tony cocked his head toward Morgan and interjected with a thin smile, "That's because you're wearing loafers, Morgan."

Tony paused for a moment, looked him in the eyes and continued, "Malcolm Forbes had a famous quote that people focus way too much on what they aren't and not enough on who or what they are. I'm not saying you should become arrogant, or conceited, or over confident - a bit less of all of that would likely be good for you, you know - I'm just saying you have a gift and you should use it."

"I do use it, when it works. It just… I don't know. It's hard to explain."

Tony paused with mild exasperation, "Look, I'm just saying you should be more open about it and sort-a advertise it. Maybe you've been looking at the Skycrane for the wrong work, maybe you should think about salvage work instead of air conditioners. Give it some thought anyway."

Morgan looked at him grimly, wondering how he was going to pay for the maintenance on the big helicopter, the insurance, the mortgage and give Melissa her half. He nodded for a moment, then turned to look out the window as the airplane accelerated then lifted off the runway.

Chapter 7 - Out With The Old

Maria Lopez gently, methodically, swept strands of her smooth, dark brown hair away from her crystal blue eyes, momentarily wrinkled her pixie like nose at the fresh smell of the bright green plants around her, blinked slowly and, again, focused through the rifle scope's eyepiece, blinking twice again to make sure her eyes were moist and clear.

She consciously calmed her breathing from long experience and focused her mind as she had done the many dozens of times before. She carefully aimed the ancient WWII German Mauser Kar 98 k sniper rifle at the target a scant 721 meters away, peering down from her hilltop perch at the small, hobby vineyard, below. This was nearly always her preferred weapon of choice. She pressed her index finger against the edge of the metal trigger guard.

With a slight smile beginning to curl the edges of her full lips, she moved her finger in and gently caressed the thin, well-worn, half round trigger. The big gun bucked hard against her padded shoulder as the large 7.92mm by 57mm lead slug screamed out of the barrel at nearly 760 meters per second. She quickly settled the barrel back down, looked back through and re-centered her scope on the target.

She watched as the man's arms puffed out when the bullet drilled in the left center of his back and the hollow headed lead round exploded out the front of his chest.

Her now EX-husband fell face first from the impact, thrown forward, his chest exploded out the front, dead before he hit the ground.

She smiled pleasantly, then smiled fiercely, "Good, now that's a proper divorce!" The abusive, arrogant bastard was gone. Grandpa Schmid would have been proud. Ernesto was just a means to an end. His well connected family was all that she wanted. He had delivered the one thing she needed, the one name and the one phone number of his contact in Washington.

She would play the role of the grieving widow with his arrogant family. And if the little airplane really held the secret box her Grandpa had wanted, she would finally be able to gain the retribution he had so desperately wanted for their family against the Venezuelan aristocracy that had looked down and persecuted them and their German heritage. She smiled smugly with her promise to get into the little airplane and secure the small box to use it as he had shared with her all those years ago before he died.

She quietly stood up and carefully, methodically, brushed her jeans off and then calmly removed a small nit of lint on her pale yellow blouse. She picked up the pure white, cotton bath towel she had been laying on and kicked over the small pile of wood she used as a rest, then carefully repacked the rifle into her dark, gray vinyl hard case, locking it tight. She laid her hand on the scratched and worn exterior of the gun case with fondness.

Maria paused to think back at her marriage to Ernesto. She had married into his wealthy family for the money. She had done terrible things to make that happen. But then Ernesto had found out about her German heritage and that she was a Schmid. He was preparing to tell his aristocratic family that he would seek a divorce from her. Her plan had always been to infiltrate the local snobbish elite, but he was about to end that. So, she provided the divorce her way.

She smiled thinly as she looked at her hastily written contact list, just one name and one phone number, some Americano intelligence twerp named Jorge or George. She paused to look out at the small valley below, then nodded with a growing smile. He'll be needing a new contact in Venezuela now for his team. She smiled broadly and picked up her cell phone from her purse to tap the phone number, her hands rock steady.

She still felt slightly flushed from the thrill of the kill as she always did. The phone call began to connect and ring.

Chapter 8 - A Meeting

Maria Lopez sat at the cafe table waiting for her American contact to show up.

She reverently re-read her Grandfather's journal papers. His meticulous handwriting on the old, yellowed and heavily creased journal pages perfectly described his anger, frustration and the persecution his family had received by the local merchants and shipping owners - the city's wealthy elite that looked down on the German foreigners who tried to buy their way into the local aristocracy after the war.

His carefully written prose described the death of his brother while attempting to apprehend the criminals who stole his papers and his most prized possession, the wooden box with the special detonator.

She read the detailed description of the secret American Treaty, the mineral map and the instructions for the German bomb. Maria smiled for a moment with a small gleam in her eye as she reread the next part of the journal. The little airplane took off that night, killed his brother with its propeller and flew into the night. Only weeks later did he hear that the little plane had never landed at the Torres estate in the North.

He spent the next decades searching and looking for the wreckage of the little plane consumed by the intense desire to regain the secret papers and the timer of the enormous German weapon. Maria looked out at the street in reflection. Getting that wooden box and timer was a perfect way to get even with the nasty and arrogant elite.

She knew what she needed to do. Get that box and use the bomb.

If the other papers were also in the plane, she realized she could use them as a way to make more money for her family. She smiled thinly, the United States leaders would desperately want to buy that treaty just to prevent it from being seen by their European partners.

Yes, she had a plan, but she needed to get to the plane first and to pull out the wooden box with the special detonator and the oilskin covered documents. Will they have survived these years in the jungle or will they be useless and destroyed. Only her resolve to get to them first and not let anything get in her way would enable her to do that.

Maria re-read these parts carefully again and again as she had so often done these past weeks. A large, black Land Rover pulled up at the cafe. She quickly closed the journal and tucked it neatly into her large purse.

Four men stepped out of the car, 3 were tall, broad shouldered and young. The fourth was thinner and older with prematurely graying hair. She looked over his team as he walked up to her. "Senora Lopez?"

"Si… yes. Are you Senor Bolton?" She responded carefully with an intentional submissiveness in her voice.

"Yes. I am sorry to hear about your loss. Why did you wish to meet? Ernesto's death has left me in a terrible situation. I wish I could say and do more to help you but Ernesto was assisting me with a special project and I now need to find a way to replace him urgently. I am sorry to say I cannot stay long and need to go soon."

"Senor Bolton, that is why I called you and why I am here. My husband suspected there were rebels in the area, but we thought we wouldn't be attacked." She dabbed her eyes again. "As you know we have a guiding business that is used by Federales and tourists."

She wiped her eyes in mock sorrow as she talked with him. "All I know is this guiding business and helping to lead tourists through dangerous lands, taking them through safely. That is what we did. Now I don't know how to keep it going and how to make any money."

George was flustered and perplexed, his chief guide was dead, apparently killed by rebels that shouldn't have been in this area South of Caracas to begin with. It just didn't make any sense. Now he was without a chief guide to work with the local team and to help ferry equipment and supplies into the deep, recovery area at an incredibly difficult and sensitive time in the op. This couldn't have happened at a worse time. He didn't want to take on and share any more information, but he also needed someone to lead the others into the salvage site and help them get there safely.

He looked at her with her pleading look and finally broke his long silence, "I am very sorry for you loss Senora Lopez. Your husband was doing some guide work for me. I'll continue to pay if you will keep the same work schedule and lead the new team in. I need to make sure the the teams and our gear continues to make it through safely. Are you able to do that?"

"Yes, Senor Bolton, I will do that and will make sure to keep to your schedule. I am familiar with the work my husband was doing. I'll lead your team in and make sure the supplies reach there destination timely and safely."

"Great, do you know where he was going or do you need a map?"

"He told me that he was going almost straight south to the Orinoco, uh… East of La Macanilla. But he didn't tell me what he was looking for…"

"I will provide a map. We found an old airplane that crashed after World War Two. Our job is to salvage the plane, the remains of the pilot if possible and contents, and to take it home." George paused for a moment, "There really isn't a lot of value in it, just one family's desire to bring home their daughter for a decent burial with her possessions."

She smiled confidently. "I can help with that. I also know brothers who are very good at salvaging found items in the jungle. I will bring them at no cost and then if they can help you, we can work out payment for their work. They work hard and are very honest."

George thought for a moment, not liking the growing hoard of people involved in what he had wanted to be a secret recovery operation. But, speed was key. He nodded "Okay. I also have a team from the U. S. military that will be arriving soon as well as an American salvage team. I'll give them your cell number to coordinate their gear and arrival.

Chapter 9 - The Ravine

Morgan and Tony just looked solemnly at each other as the older model Toyota Land Cruiser bounced them jarringly over the rough, dirt road, approaching the new and makeshift work site. They had traveled from La Estacada in the Southern part of the country to a small, raging tributary just North of the Meta River. The part of the tributary they were above was very high and situated in a deep, narrow ravine completely covered by dense jungle, except for the shrub and grass covered field they were now parked at.

Morgan frowned as he looked out at the two groups of men clearly separated and working apart. One team of Hispanic men were at the edge of a ravine at the end of a short, grass and mud expanse, completely surrounded by dense, dark jungle trees. They were rushing to pull up a rope, intent on what was going on underneath the sharp edge of the cliff.

The engine of the Land Cruiser stopped and was instantly replaced by the loud cacophony of sound filling their ears. The birds, monkeys and incredible wealth of animal and insect life made their presence known. The deep, earthy smell of jungle, mud and strange flowers permeated their senses.

Morgan lurched out of the SUV and looked around to take in the sights, sounds, smells and essence of the jungle. He closed his eyes for a moment to help him concentrate on the life and dense vegetation that surrounded them. This odd habit helped him to quickly orient to his environment and had saved his life more than once.

He looked up at the slightly over cast, morning air, already well over 80 degrees Fahrenheit. Morgan did that math in his head… more than 27 Celsius. He was already sweating from the humid heat and the nearly 20 kilometer nerve-wracking drive through the jungle to get here. He surveyed the surrounding landscape of grassy and scrub brush covered meadow surrounded by dense jungle as if to fix it in his mind, then turned toward the bustle of human activity to his right with the two separate groups of men going about their frantic work.

Morgan and Tony went around the back, opened the rear hatch and removed their stuffed day-packs. Morgan pushed his elbow against Tony's arm and looked down at the blanket covering the gear in the back of the vehicle. The edge of the blanket had shifted up and the front of the scratched and dented hard case, handle and label showed. The small label said 'Schmid'. While her back was to them, Morgan deftly popped both latches and gently lifted the top exposing the Mauser sniper rifle. He quickly closed and re-latched it before she turned around. Morgan quickly recovered the case with the blanket then stepped away. Tony simply nodded as Morgan carefully closed the hatch and lifted their day packs to their shoulders.

Their female driver, Maria Lopez, had briskly exited the car. She was arguing and gesticulating to a wiry, somber, older Caucasian man with thinning gray hair, in a sweat stained cream colored, long sleeve shirt and very wrinkled tan slacks, standing between the two groups. She was clearly agitated pointing to the Hispanic team, then the other team under the broad canopy and toward the new arrivals, Tony and Morgan. She was clearly not happy - that had been very evident from their entire trip in. She was very angry and resented Morgan and Tony being added to the already crowded group of salvage experts.

With a short, curt response, the Caucasian ended the discussion and quickly walked over to greet them shaking Tony's hand, then Morgan's. "Hello again Tony. It has been a long time. Let's get started."

Tony, nodded and began to motion toward Morgan when he interrupted and continued, "I want to give you a short situation report and have you get to work right away." He turned to Morgan, "I recognize you from your file, Mr. Fox. You've done some impressive work in the middle east. I have to say, I was both surprised and impressed by your recent find in Canada this week. That was smart. Clearly no one else thought to look up or that a plane could crash into the top of a tree and stay there."

Morgan looked firmly, intently at him, surprised at his knowing about the Canadian operation, "And you are?"

"I'm George Bolton, leading this recovery effort, Mr. Fox. I thought you knew that."

"Tony mentioned you would be leading the effort and that he'd done some work for you before, but really didn't describe you in a lot of detail or that you'd be on-site."

George frowned for a moment, then went on. "Yes, well, that was a different time and something we can't go into. What do you both need here to get started? As you can see, we have two other teams working to get down to the plane. It is over the edge..." George pointed straight out where the Hispanic men were clamoring around urgently trying to get at something or pull something up. "Our Hispanic team just lost another member if my Spanish is good enough to understand what just happened. This is the 2nd member of their team to die. Three others have been seriously injured. The Brag team has not fared much better." George motioned glumly to the Americans standing under the canopy cover. "They've lost one member as well."

Tony turned to George while he cocked his head to one side, "What do you mean 'lost'?"

George turned back to face Morgan and Tony, "Exactly what I said. The American team had a climber down near the airplane and something happened to his climbing line. He fell to his death and the body is somewhere down stream." He waved generally down to their left and continued, "There is a waterfall directly under us as well as rapids both above the waterfall and after it. We have no way of getting to the body even if we could search and find it." George paused for a moment in reflection, "Mr. Fox…"

"Call me Morgan." Interrupted Morgan.

"Ah, okay… Morgan. Tony shared your very strong 'finding' skills. Which we clearly do not need here. But he also shared your exceptional recovery skills - your, how should I say this… creative way, of recovering downed aircraft in the Middle-East. I am impressed by that work. That is why I asked him to bring you in. Now, gentlemen, what do you need to proceed, because clearly our teams need the help."

Morgan paused, looked at Tony who was grimly surveying the work in front of them, "I'd like us to look around, try to get to a point to see the airplane, what type it is, orientation, that kind of thing. What is the timeline?"

George smiled thinly, "The plane is a 1939 Ercoupe, single engine, low wing monoplane. It is wedged in the chasm between the two walls of the ravine about 150 feet down. The reason it has been hidden so long is that this is, as you may have surmised, a remote region of Venezuela and the plane is not visible from above. There are two separated, over-hangs that prevent direct observation. No one has made it to the plane yet, at least three have died trying, due to the chaotic, high wind, sharp, difficult rock and difficult access. I'm not sure of the complete context, but the lead Brag climber described the rock as 'manky'. That does not sound good to me."

George paused, "The urgency is that we need the plane, pilot and bits out now, quickly and as soon as we can. It is extremely urgent. Why that is important is classified. I know we are a long way from home, but this is a national security issue for the United States that is compounded by the sensitivity that we are in a foreign country that does not know we are here doing this work. And, they cannot ever know that we are here doing this work. Do you understand?"

Tony finally broke his silence, "We get that George, otherwise there wouldn't be a need for you to be here."

"Correct. Let me know what you need. Maria is my liaison to the Hispanic team. She will coordinate directly or with me to get whatever equipment you need." George looked at his watch and began to walk off toward the big canopy. "My Brag meeting is now. I'll set up a schedule for us to review progress."

Morgan interrupted him, "George, why do you call them the brag team?"

George turned as he walked away. "I'm sure Tony already told you I brought in a Spec Ops team from Ft. Brag to help with the recovery and… other security related matters." He turned and kept walking away.

Morgan turned to Tony shaking his head, "None of this makes any sense. Why the urgency after all of these years? Why bring in a team from Ft. Brag? What is so urgent that he has not one, not two, but three teams COMPETING to get to the plane. That is just plain bad news. What the hell is going on here?"

Tony continued to survey the army special forces team and then the Hispanic salvage team as he slowly responded, "None of this makes sense. When he called me, he didn't share any of this. He mentioned he was also looking at a Spec Ops team with expertise, but he didn't tell me he actually brought them in or that there was another group. Morg, I'm just guessing that the urgency is that everything was fine UNTIL the plane was found and no one the wiser. Now the plane is found and there is extreme urgency to get it out."

Morgan thought reflectively for a moment, then cocked his head to one side, staring out at the two teams very clearly separated from each other.

"Tony… maybe it ISN'T the plane. Maybe it is the person or what they carried in the plane. You said before, he wanted to salvage the plane, pull it out with what was inside, emphasis on what was inside. That is key, I think. He said it is a '39 Ercoupe. That is a pretty small plane as I recall, so it can't be big and bulky - one or two people with very small, very special cargo."

Morgan walked around to the front of the Land Cruiser and sat against the smooth chrome bumper and grill, looking at the urgent activity by the Hispanic team and the completely separate work area of the American Army team. He shook his head again and stopped, not liking the feeling. His quasi 6th sense was ringing in his head and not in a good way. None of this made sense. You just don't run an operation like this. There were too many people and too many teams.

Tony, looked around at the work area, the cars and truck, his hand sweeping the vista. "Morgan, what else do you see?"

Staring ahead without looking over at Tony, Morgan quickly responded, "No tents, no trucks, no anything. This is all temporary and any support is all off-site, likely back in La Estacada."

"Right, this is all a temporary, day-time only op."

Morgan nodded glumly, shaking his head, "They commute in and out each day. So odd. If there was so much urgency, why not camp here? Make it a 24 hour day. Why no guards? No drones, no electronic surveillance, that I can see. None of this makes any sense, Tony. Unless, we can't stay at night because of the security issue. I wonder if that is why the Brag team is here. Maybe there are rebels near by? This is just so weird."

Chapter 10 - An Evaluation And A Revelation

The next morning just after 8 AM, Morgan and Tony arrived on-site with Maria Lopez in the Land Cruiser.

The Brag crew and Hispanic team had not arrived yet. The sun was up, it was already hot and humid, with a clear, blue sky. The air smelled of detritus and dead plants. The mosquitoes were already out in force, hunting for prey.

George was not around either.

Her mood had not improved. She remained hostile, angry and belligerent. Both the Brag team and, now, Tony and Morgan clearly did not fit in her plan. It was evident she much preferred working with the Hispanic team to try and reach the plane.

They walked over to the edge while Maria waited next to the car for the two other crews. Morgan stood at the edge and turned to Tony, "Does it feel like the wind is less turbulent this morning?"

"Morgan, I don't know, I don't have a good sense for that. What are you thinking?"

"Yesterday afternoon, when we met with George, he mentioned the teams come in about 8 AM to make sure there is sunlight on the road and safe to travel. I'm wondering if the wind is variable based on the time of day and temperature. I know we are a long way from the coast. Hmm, I wonder if the flat-lands out to the East near the Orinoco create any kind of wind flow or buffer that changes the wind strength or direction based on time of day. If they haven't checked this, we should."

Tony responded, "Morg, it makes sense, but where are you going with this?"

"Remember yesterday afternoon when the Brag team was all excited. They pulled up one of their guys with a broken arm and he was excited that he actually saw the airplane? Do you remember that?"

"Yes and George was excited they saw it too."

Morgan continued, "Tony, if the waterfalls and wind, create this constant, heavy, billowing mist, then who found the airplane and how did they do that? If these expert climbers can't get down to the plane and no one can see it because of this heavy mist, HOW did someone find it, Tony, hmmm?" Morgan just shook his head, perplexed and still processing the situation.

Tony turned toward him and just looked eyes wide at Morgan's obvious question.

Tony looked at Morgan and down into the chasm with the billowing and windy mist created from the cascading waterfall. The billowing, thick, turbulent mists swirled up from the frothy falls and began to dissipate only 5 meters from the cliff top.

Morgan looked over at Tony, then the trucks with the two arriving teams, then back at Tony, "We need our own jeep or 4 wheel drive. I don't like being dependent on her. She clearly does not like us being here and I'd prefer not to share our plans and work with her. Something about her just doesn't fit."

Tony turned to Morgan, "Is that your 6th sense talking? Or, you just don't like her?"

Morgan smiled thinly for a moment, "I'm not sure about either, but all of this doesn't feel right and she doesn't feel right either." He paused looking out at the jungle and then back at the approaching teams. "I don't know, I guess I just like us to have freedom of movement and control of our own time. It would enable us to arrive earlier or stay later to see what the wind in the ravine is doing. Since you know George better…"

Tony smiled broadly and interrupted, "…yes, I'll ask him to get us a jeep or Land Cruiser. Since I'm making a list, what else will we need? These groups have a ton of climbing gear, ropes, pitons, technical gear and… oh yeah, lot's of gung-ho attitude. What do we need that they don't already have?"

It was Morgan's turn to smile, "I'm thinking a different approach. They are clearly all expert at rock climbing so they got that covered. They are Army and well trained for security. Why don't we try a different approach. Keep it between us for now, but we may need to get a larger 4 wheel drive truck, something heavier, with a big cable winch. I haven't seen one of those yet so they may not have thought about it. And, Tony, at some point we may need to source our own local guide. Someone who knows this area, the jungle and river."

"You mean like a winch to pull up the actual airplane? Hmm, maybe his instructions to them are different than ours. Maybe he told them to just get the stuff out of the airplane - no need to salvage."

"All the more reason this just doesn't make sense. 'Just such a cluster…"

As Morgan finished his comment, George drove up in a jeep with 4 other men who looked a lot like body guards. The two groups went to their specific spots to begin their day.

George strode over to Tony and Morgan and motioned them further away. "Gentlemen, we have a problem."

Tony looked up with a serious face,"What's up?"

"I need you guys to find a way to get into the plane quickly."

"What happened? You said it was urgent before, what has made it worse."

"Two things. While you were flying down here, we began to hear rumors of someone starting to seek interest in bartering or brokering an old document that would prove to be very sensitive and embarrassing to the U.S."

He paused for a moment, "If someone knows what's in the plane, that can blow the lid off this entire operation and expose... well, expose something we can't afford to be public."

Tony asked with a perplexed look, "So why are you sharing this - why are you trusting us?"

Morgan interjected, "Because he hasn't told us what the document is, so there is no way we could be the agent provocateur trying to sell this stuff."

Tony gently shook his head and rolled his eyes, "Doh, I didn't connect those dots."

George continued, "That's correct, you are both in the clear because I never told you what it is. What is very strange and scary is that other than our department, Director and our President, no one should know what is in the plane. Which brings me to point number two. Do either of you have any contact with Senator Adam Cole?"

Morgan turned to Tony, "I don't. I think I've heard the name on the news but have never contacted him or been contacted by him. Tony?"

"Me neither. George, what's up?"

George paused for a moment with his lips pursed, thinking, "Senator Cole is not and should not be a part of the recovery. He shouldn't even know about it or what we are trying to recover. Yet, he called my office and demanded an update on our progress, where we were, who was involved and what they were doing. He was pretty belligerent and forceful about it. My senior aide was successful in deflecting the issue, but it is clear he knows enough to be dangerous and is demanding to be kept informed. It is imperative he not become aware of or receive possession of the material in the plane. I am sharing that from a national security perspective but can't go further than that. I am actually surprised he even knew about the plane and our work down here."

Morgan looked at him seriously, "So, George. What's in it?"

George paused, scrunched his lips together, then added, "This is all completely top secret. It is a secret document from WW2 that should never see the light of day. It would permanently ruin our relationships with several close partners. That's all you need to know. Now, let's get to work. We need to get into the plane!"

The day would not turn out well… the wet, turbulent, volatile winds in the gorge would claim two more lives, one from each camp.

Chapter 11 - Independence

At the hotel, they stepped out the front door as Maria drove up. Morgan stepped around to her open window, "Tony and I have some other work we need to attend to today so are not going out to the site."

She simply nodded with no evident emotion and put the car in gear. Morgan quickly stepped out of her way to not get run over.

Tony called George, "George, we will be late today. We are going to rent our own car so we don't have to rely on Maria. It will give us some flexibility to work out a solution on our own."

"Okay Tony, if that is what you need to move this forward, it is approved. Use Martinez Rental in town. Alejandro Martinez owns it and has been providing equipment for our effort. I have an account with him."

Tony ended the call and put his phone in his pocket. He looked over at Morgan who still had an odd, uncertain look.

"What's up, Morg. I know that expression and it usually isn't good."

Morgan frowned, "I get that paying us what he agreed to isn't usual. It's a lot of money, especially since we already know where the plane is. I understand that doing this salvage work in another country brings its own element of risk. But this feels way over the top of that. There is a lot more going on that I just can't figure out yet."

Tony just looked at him, thin lipped. He'd known Morgan for a decade and knew Morgan's instinct and sixth sense was unusually good... often very, very good.

Morgan quickly glanced away looking down the street, shaking his head, "And, we have a tail."

Tony didn't bother to look, that would just warn the tail he or she had been made. Instead, he waived his hand and flagged down a taxi. They both climbed into the back of the sedan telling the driver where to take them. It dropped them off in front of the Martinez rental company.

Tienda de Alquiler de Martínez was a large, sprawling, walled in commercial equipment rental yard in town with a heavy iron gate in front, with busy one story offices just inside the gate and a large selection of equipment, cargo shipping containers, trucks, rental cars, construction equipment, generators, ladders of all sizes and portable lighting systems covering the huge yard.

There also were several outbuildings for other equipment, ongoing maintenance and storage. Workers were everywhere, moving equipment, cleaning returned equipment and making repairs.

The guys walked through the gate and went inside the office. The main desk was in front. Behind was a big open area with many shelves filled with construction, painting and maintenance equipment.

A smiling young man looked up from the counter, "Hola, como puedo ayudarte?"

Morgan smiled quickly, "May we see Senor Martinez, another customer of his suggested we come here."

The young man nodded then added in perfect English, "Of course, one moment please." He stepped into a nearby office and spoke briefly. A slender man dressed in brown slacks with a pressed white cotton shirt stepped around his desk and came out.

"Hello, I am Alejandro Martinez. And you are?"

"I'm Morgan Fox and this is Tony Fisher. George Bolton suggested we come here."

Alejandro motioned them around the counter to his office. "Please sit. Would you like water?"

They both declined.

Alejandro sat down, his face a serious mask, "Gentlemen, how is the plane recovery going?"

Both Tony and Morgan were startled.

Morgan asked, "How do you know about that?"

"Everyone here knows about that, including the U. S. Army team and out team of workers". He smiled for a moment then added, "There are few foreigners that come to La Estacada, so when an American business man visits and brings a U. S. Army team with him... people take notice."

He noticed the serious expression on the faces, then motioned with his hand, "Please don't worry, the information doesn't go anywhere. The people here are loyal to our town family. We know who is in the little plane and many of our local citizens are related to the Torres family and to Isabella herself. That is why they volunteered to help and work with Senora Lopez to try and recover the plane and the body of Senorita Torres. Now, gentlemen, how may I assist you today?"

Morgan and Tony looked at each other for a moment. Morgan nodded and began, "Thank you for sharing that. Yes, we are here to help retrieve the plane. We didn't realize we all were so obvious."

Morgan paused for a moment, "Senor Martinez, it sounds like you know about the plane and where it is. Have you seen the plane?"

Alejandro responded, "Yes, my family has known about the plane since it disappeared. My Uncle found the plane about 40 years ago. That is why we moved here, to be closer to her until we could bring her home. My Uncle took me the long way around to the other side of the river and we were able to get close enough to see inside with binoculars. We have never been able to get any closer to her."

Morgan looked puzzled, "If you haven't been close to the plane, has anyone actually approached it?"

"No one has been able to get to it. We have also tried the same trick of using ropes to climb down. That is how my Uncle died. We also tried rafts to navigate the terrible rapids both from above and below the waterfalls. That is how my brother died. So, no… no one has actually been able to find a way to get to the plane. Otherwise we would have retrieved Isabella a long time ago."

Tony looked confused, "I don't understand, if you haven't been close to the plane how did our gov… I mean Mr. Bolton find out about it?"

Alejandro Martinez laughed out loud, then looked at both of them with a dead pan, serious expression, "I don't know. I asked Senor Bolton that but he wouldn't give me a direct answer. Now, I will help you and ask only one favor."

Tony asked, "What is that?"

"We do not know you. I do not know you... but I will risk being obvious for the sake of our Isabella. I ask you to bring back the remains of our dear Isabella for a proper burial. I ask you to recover her with the care and respect she deserves. I am her nephew and our family would be thankful. Now, gentlemen, what equipment do you need."

Morgan smiled, "That is our goal as well. Right now we want to rent a vehicle, like a Land Cruiser or something similar that is 4 wheel drive or all wheel drive, rugged and reliable."

Senor Martinez looked over at them slightly confused, "Will this help recover Isabella? Is this for the same work Senor Bolton is doing?"

"Yes it is. We feel we need the flexibility to travel to and from the site when needed and to not have to depend on Maria Lopez. George shared that he has an account with you."

"Then that is fine." Alejandro paused, then added pointing toward the parking lot, "We have that slightly rough but very strong and reliable Land Cruiser parked outside."

He got up and motioned them to walk out with him. He reached into a drawer at the counter and pulled out a set of keys, handing them to Morgan. "Here you are. You are all set. I'll add this to Senor Bolton's account. Gentlemen, thank you and have a good day."

Tony looked at Morgan then at Senor Martinez, "Do we have to fill out paperwork or sign any document?"

Senor Martinez paused and shrugged, "You can if you prefer, but I don't need you to. This is not America. Here, we do business based on the strength of our honor. I am trusting you now. You both look like honorable men and you are doing work for Senor Bolton. That is good enough for me. Please bring Isabella back to us."

Alejandro walked around his desk and turned to face them directly, his face a mask of solemn seriousness, "If there becomes a time when you may need other equipment or supplies to assist with the recovery, please… please do not hesitate to ask me for that. I would gladly help. I just hope you can bring our Isabella home."

Chapter 12 - Discovery

Maria stepped into the now, long empty warehouse her family had owned these many years.

She pulled out the well worn journal from her Grandfather and reread the detailed instructions describing the underground location of the German bomb her grandfather and grand uncle had brought with them at the end of the war.

She looked across the open space to see if there were any signs of intruders or habitation. Finding none, she slung the heavy burlap sack over her shoulder. She walked quietly across the vast open and empty warehouse.

Dim light filtered through the high windows above her and at the top of the side walls. Dirt, litter, old pallets and rotting boxes littered all over the dusty warehouse floor.

Off the center of the open space were the walled offices. She carefully stepped her way over to them through the scattered piles of pallets and boxes, and walked around. She was surprised that the glass windows were intact. Maria looked in the offices at the now barren work spaces.

She reached inside the door then turned on the light switch and was momentarily startled. The power was still on. Several incandescent light bulbs brightened the otherwise shadowy space.

Maria stepped out of the office space then walked around the back of the offices exploring the solid wall and the covered air vent mentioned in the journal. She reached up and could just touch the bottom of the vent. The covered vent screen was still solid and intact. She dropped her burlap bag next to the brick wall.

Maria looked around and pulled an open wooden crate over. She turned it on its side, then climbed up to pull open the vent grate. It wouldn't budge. Maria pulled out her small, powerful battery operated headlamp, put it on with the lamp on her forehead and pressed the on button. A bright light lit the grate and interior. she could see inside as the vent was big enough to stand up in once inside.

She carefully looked for a latch and found it inside on the middle of the left side of the grate. It took her a couple of minutes fiddling with it to figure out how to push, slide and then pop out the little lever. She pressed it to the side and felt a click as the little latch let go.

She carefully stepped back on the edge of the crate and pulled the vent frame open. It moved slowly and with a lot of resistance, but made little noise. She used her headlamp to look inside for any traps or other levers. The journal didn't warn of any but she was cautious and wanted to make sure she would not trip some kind of trap or device.

Maria took a moment to look around, grabbed her heavy burlap bag, pushed it in to the vent in front of her and lifted herself into the vent.

Once inside she stood up in the large opening.

Out of cautious fear, she pulled the vent almost closed, grabbed her bag and turned around to explore the interior. The floor and walls were all mortared brick and solid under foot. A thin layer of dust covered the floor that stayed on it as she moved and didn't puff up.

The air was surprisingly comfortable to breath with just a hint of movement. She stopped for a moment, that must mean there is another vent or air source somewhere.

She looked at the small space and saw the narrow vent tunnel turn to her left. She looked at the floor and looked around the corner and instantly smiled. There in front of her were the steps leading down to the secret basement. She looked around once more, then quickly behind her and then carefully stepped forward, around the corner and started down the stairs. Maria stepped slowly and carefully, looking all around her at the walls, top and steps of the staircase as she stepped down about 7 meters.

The end of the stairs opened up into a large separate room she estimated as 10 meters by 15 meters with a ceiling of 4 meters.

Using her headlamp, she looked around and found another light switch. Doubting it would work down here, she was pleasantly surprised when she flipped the switch and 4 ceiling mounted bulbs lit.

She sniffed for a moment. The air was still clean and seemingly fresh. Almost no dust covered the floor.

She pulled the old journal out of her small daypack and reread it again. Straight to her right from the stairs was the brick wall she was looking for. She looked at the heavy wood beams above her and made her way over to the brick wall.

If she read the journal correctly, the big bomb was behind it. She smiled in anticipation.

Maria scanned the completely empty room. It was devoid of any trash or junk. She ran her hands and fingers over the brick and mortar. The wall felt very solid. She looked up at the top of the wall. The brick stopped at the beam. Her light made it appear as though there was a very narrow gap of a couple of centimeters at the very top. She paused for a moment, maybe that meant the basement was built first, the big bomb set in, the large warehouse floor constructed and then the closing brick wall erected after? She ran her hand over the brick wall again.

Shaking her head to herself, she turned and went back up the stairs, stopped at the vent entry to quietly survey the interior of the warehouse. It was still empty and quiet.

She hoisted her burlap bag, grunted under the weight of it and carried it down into the basement to the base of the wall.

She took a moment to reread the journal and then pulled out the large sledge hammer. She carefully hoisted it over her shoulder, took a deep breath lifted and then slammed it down onto the brick wall. The sound of the strike thundered in the small space. Mortar dust puffed off of the wall, but nothing else happened. With gritty determination, she reached back into the sack, pulled out a painters mask, a pair of plastic safety glasses and heavy gloves.

Maria then pulled a tie out of her pocket and used it to tie her hair back and out of the way. Taking one more look at the wall, she went to work.

Almost two hours later, incredible tired and covered in sweat, dust and grime, she stopped and smiled under her stained mask. She had broken enough of a hole to look inside the wall.

Maria used her headlamp to peer in and saw a large, rounded shape, about the size of a small family car, covered in heavy, dark cloth sheets.

A few more heavy hits with her sledge hammer and she opened enough of a hole to duck in to. Maria threw bricks off to the side to make it easier to get in, then ducked under the now sagging and leaning, but still stable wall opening. One anemic light bulb still shown faintly inside, powered by the same wires that fed the other lights in the rest of the basement. She ducked inside barely able to contain her excitement but also careful to not touch the leaning wall in case that would affect its stability.

The inside of the enclosed room was as wide as the outside of the basement. The builders had started with a much bigger room, set the device on one side then simply built a stacked brick and mortar wall up to the beam ceiling to close it off from the outside world.

Even with the one bulb the shadows were deep and eerie.

There was little air movement inside. The dust hung in the air like a dim fog.

She turned her head toward the device and her head lamp illuminated the dark green canvas cover. Maria paused cautiously and looked around the perimeter for signs of traps or wires. Finding none, she walked up to the device, grabbed one corner of the canvas and began to roll it up with growing excitement to uncover the device underneath. She kept rolling it up, smiling gleefully under her mask, and completely uncovered the bomb.

This was the bomb and it was huge. It was a large, car-sized cylinder sitting on two large metal rails, one on each side of the device. The ends of the bomb were rounded hemispheres. The entire bomb had been painted a dull, deep gray-blue. On her side next to the hole in the wall she came in through was a single metal box riveted to the side of the cylinder. Maria quickly moved to it. She looked it over with her headlamp and felt around the outside for the latch. Her hands felt the simple mechanism at the bottom of the box, so she unlatched the bottom of the cover and opened it a short distance. The painted sheet metal cover moved easily and soundlessly as though it had been just finished. Her light shown on the hinge now covered with dust. She could see dark grease in the hinge and smiled at the meticulousness of her grandfather. She opened the cover all the way up and saw the single, round cavity meant for the detonator. That was all there was to it. It was a very simple device to her, just a spot to set the detonator in, screw it down and be done. She looked more carefully at the cavity and saw a loosely coiled wire cable with a connector on the end.

Maria smiled grimly, knowing this was her tool for revenge and reinforced her mission to get to the airplane, the wood box and the detonator.

Chapter 13 - Enlightenment

Tony turned to Morgan as he left the hotel lobby front door. "Several days ago, you mentioned we had a tail. Is it that gray haired guy behind us who is trying not to be noticed in his Hawaiian shirt and khaki pants?"

"Nope, it is the guy in front of us about a block down on the other side of the street with the tan jacket and black pants. I don't get these people. Who taught them to wear a jacket when it's like more than 30 Celsius here?"

Since they were walking forward anyway, Tony gently turned his head to the right but quickly glanced left down the street, hoping his gaze would not spook the tail. "Ah, got it."

Morgan kept walking straight on down the street already crowded with local citizens going about their daily work. "It's odd Tony. I feel like this place is getting crowded with spooks. Why are we attracting all of this attention?"

"I don't know but it's odd. If they are working together, they are doing an absolutely lousy job of coordinating their surveillance."

"Or worse, they are not the same team. I think it is time to try and determine who they are. You okay with that?"

"Both? Really?"

"Well, okay, we'll start with this one in front and work from there. He seems like a rank amateur wearing that stupid jacket. I think we split up and try and do a high/low on him like we did in Kabul."

"We'll need an alley that has a wall to make that work. Are you the bait this time?"

Morgan quipped with a perfectly dead-pan face, "Nope, you are and I found you the alley. Look up there across the street, a tight alley with a dumpster that even I can hide behind."

Morgan looked quickly both ways to make sure there was no traffic then he joined the handful of pedestrians casually crossing the street. He kept looking for their forward tail to make sure he was watching them. He was clearly an amateur. He would actually look at them every few seconds to see where they went.

Morgan looked to the side keeping his face forward to see more about their antagonist. He was clearly ex-military in his stance and short dark haircut, but had also gained some weight that would slow him down.

"Remind me the next time we see George to ask him for hardware or something to use for protection. This is all going to be close in and hand to hand. If he has a gun and it looks like he may have since he has that stupid jacket on in this heat, it is going to be risky to disarm him, even in the alley."

"Got it. Note to self, harass George for weaponry."

Morgan smiled for just a moment.

They walked up on the thin sidewalk and meandered toward the alley. Morgan intentionally looked carefully into the street to signal any pursuers that they were wanting to enter the alley without being seen. He hoped the tail would be curious at their actions.

They both entered the alley and Morgan quickly ducked behind the garbage dumpster. It was faded blue with large dents and many rust spots from years of hard use… and it stunk with the stench of old and decaying food. A thin, wet pool of viscous slime puddled out from a corner hole.

Morgan tucked back against the red brick wall and the inside corner of the dumpster.

Tony hugged the wall and slowly made his way down the alley toward another dumpster about a hundred feet further on.

He moved slowly in hopes that the tail would follow him in.

Sure enough, the man with the tan jacket peered around the corner. Tony could see him out of the corners of his eyes as he leaned next to the second dumpster. He started to move on toward the end and the tail followed him in. Morgan thought to himself that this one was clearly an amateur. Tony walked around the next corner wide and then quickly looped back to stay close to the wall.

The tail was uncertain what to do, but decided to move forward to see where they went. He started walking down the alley and Morgan stepped away from the wall just as he passed.

He felt Morgan's presence and saw the movement out of the corner of his eye. He reacted quickly lashing out with a knife to move Morgan back and then followed up by pulling his gun out from his back belt. The jacket caught on the hammer of the gun causing it to snag for a moment. That was enough time to cause the gunman to look down for just a second. Morgan had already moved and lept forward to grab the knife arm and twisted his hand. The gun came free as the enemy tried to twist away in surprise. He pulled the trigger too early and the shot went high and wide as he tried to aim for Morgan's chest. Morgan twisted the arm behind the gunman and jabbed the knife deep into his kidney. The man screamed and tried to twist around, but Morgan followed him around not letting him spin. He jabbed the knife hand again pushing the knife into his back under his rib cage. He screamed again and pointed the gun over his back and shoulder to shoot again. Morgan saw the gun coming over the top and used his right hand to grab the slide pushing it back to prevent it from firing. The enemy struggled to fire and to free both of his hands. He was already dying from the two knife strikes to his kidney and lower back.

Morgan felt him begin to fight less so he shoved him forward as hard as he could into the wall next to the dumpster. He pulled him back then used his left shoulder, still holding the assailants now broken left hand with the knife shoving his face and head into the wall.

Blood streamed down his back and side. He collapsed against the wall and let go of the gun.

Morgan held on to the gun so it wouldn't fall and then let the man go. Tony ran up and Morgan handed him the weapon then grabbed the knife out of the assailant's hand and handed that to Tony too. The man was clearly dying.

Morgan pulled him over. He was barely breathing.

Morgan knelt close to him, "Who are you working for. Why are you here?" The man looked at Morgan as the focus of his eyes waned.

He simply died without saying anything.

Morgan took out his phone and quickly took a picture of the man's face and then a close up of his right thumb and fingers. He quickly patted down the pockets looking for a wallet or other identification. The only thing he found was a cheap phone. He pocketed that and stood up.

He and Tony simply turned and walked back into the street as Tony threw the knife and gun into the dumpster.

Chapter 14 - Desperate Times

"Senor Bolton, these men will not go on." Maria complained with exasperation. "This task is impossible this way and they will leave. They have lost 4 men and thousands of bolivars trying to reach the little plane. This job simply cannot be done this way. We must find a different answer. Why can't we try a mobile crane or a helicopter?"

"Senora, we have been through this before." He said with exasperation. "A truck carrying any kind of crane will not make it over the jungle roads or skirting the cliff roads we use to get us here. And bringing in a helicopter with the type of winch and cable we need would attract too many questions and attention." He continued emphatically, "No, we have got to find a way with what we have."

"Senor Bolton, the men are frustrated, tired and cannot find the answer we need. I am very concerned they will leave us."

"They can't leave, the job isn't finished. The plane and its contents are still down there. I need you to talk with them, we need to at least retrieve any artifacts inside the plane even if we can't retrieve the whole airplane. That is very important. That is our deal. They get paid, YOU get paid when the job is complete."

"Senor Bolton, this will not work. They need to take a break. They have lost good men and have been at this every day for more than a month. They are all exhausted. Even your famous American Army team has made no progress and also those two from Canada. This simply cannot go on. We need a different way."

"Senora Lopez, this has to go on, this is a very important matter. Give your team a rest for a couple of days and this may help them think through a new solution. You and your team are very important to this project. You have the local knowledge and understand the terrain, the environment and the rebels. I respect the work they have done and the losses they have suffered. Take some time." He paused to consider his next step, "Will 2 days be enough or do they need more to return refreshed?"

"I will talk with them. I think 2 days is good for now, but they may want more bolivars to replace their lost equipment and for the danger this project is."

"I understand. I will pay for the equipment and we can talk later when they return about an increase in the project fee. Will that work?"

"Yes, Senor Bolton, I will have them stop for today and rest. We will be back in two days time."

"Senora Lopez, I will advise the other groups to do the same. This is a very important recovery project and I need all the teams focused."

"Senor, we do not need the other teams, they do not add value and just argue and distract from the work we are doing. Send them all home. That will make this project go easier."

"Senora, that isn't an option for us. They will stay and continue to work. All of them. Everyone has been at this and needs a short break. I'll have them also take a couple of days off, but they will return in two days time to continue to get down to the airplane. It is urgent that we complete this and get down to the plane." With that, George turned, clearly angry, and hiked backed to the Brag team to share the news they would be taking two days off.

Chapter 15 - An Opportunity Appears

Several days later, Morgan and Tony left their small hotel early and drove through town, down the highway and over the narrow, rough roads in the jungle to the ravine. They intentionally arrived much earlier than the other teams and were the only team there.

They drove right up to the cliff edge and parked. As they both got out they could see well down into the ravine, but still could not see the airplane because of how and where it was wedged between the two rock walls in the narrow ravine below.

The foggy mist and swirling wind was barely moving. They could see the faint churning river and two of the waterfalls but still could not see the plane.

Morgan looked around and walked from one side to the other trying to see in the center section where the plane was stuck. He was not successful.

He turned to Tony, shaking his head, "If we can't see it at all from here, there is no way someone discovered it from up here. Maybe there is a way down below." He sat down on the hard rock cliff edge his legs dangling over the side and looked down stream.

Tony came over and sat next to him. "What are you thinking, are we on the wrong side of the ravine to see the plane?"

"That is what Martinez said. I don't know but it doesn't make sense that someone can find the plane but we can't see it from up here." Morgan paused then continued, pointing down the river, "And look down stream, the cliff walls are vertical, well nearly so with rough boulders on either side at the bottom. No one is going to hike or climb up from below to get to this point."

Morgan got up and began walking back from the edge. Tony followed as Morgan began walking Southwest toward the upstream portion of the river and ravine. Every 3 to 4 meters he stopped to look down, but the sides of the ravine were too vertical and steep to see much. The ravine walls were fairly close together and they could easily see across to the other side. Morgan pointed to the other side, "The walls are very sheer and I don't see any sign of a path or easy way down, unless it is way up stream."

The gusting breeze was beginning to pick up, becoming stronger as the sun warmed up the sky, making it more difficult to see anywhere down into the ravine.

Morgan kept walking upstream away from the grassy meadow and into denser shrubs and jungle, stopping every few meters to look over the edge for perspective.

He made his way slowly along the edge to a point where the river curved upstream and further South. At that bend, they stopped and looked down barely seeing any part of the frothy, turbulent river.

Tony looked down, "You can't even see the plane from here. If the teams hadn't actually seen the plane, I'd say there wasn't one down there."

Morgan walked further into the heavy shrubs overhanging the ravine edge, stopped to look at Tony and then smiled broadly. "I think I know a way down."

Tony looked at him quizzically with his head cocked to one side, "How so?"

With that Morgan stepped toward the edge, around the shrub and disappeared into the chasm.

Tony was shocked, then frightened. He rushed over to the edge where Morgan had disappeared. Expecting the worst he looked out over the ravine and saw Morgan standing on a narrow, rocky path several steps down from the rim. He stepped down a couple of more steps with his left hand resting and moving along the rock wall of the ravine. He stopped quickly and looked at his watch.

They had been onsite for almost an hour and it was almost 07:45. He carefully turned around to walk back up the wall to Tony, smiling.

Tony gently shook his head and smiled. "You do have the gift Morg. You really do."

Morgan chuckled, shaking his head, "It was more of a process of elimination. Clearly what everyone has been working on hasn't worked." He smiled as he knelt down on one knee at the edge of the cliff path and pointed. "We don't know if it goes down to the bottom yet. But it certainly looks promising. See how weathered and old it looks? I think this path has been here a very long time, maybe hundreds of years and you'd never find it if you didn't already know it was here or happened to be searching the edge in those bushes."

"Let's go down and find out!"

"Not today, its too late for that, the other teams will be here shortly. Let's go back, play dumb for now and we'll come back tomorrow early again. And Tony…" He paused, "…that means we don't yet tell George."

"Okay, I like that, but why not tell George?"

"First we don't know if it goes to the bottom and second he would have the other teams immediately start to explore it. I'd like to make sure we know what we are dealing with before we disclose this. I don't know… its just a feeling. I'm still not trusting Maria and the other teams. Oh, another thing. If someone found out about the old document and is trying to shop it around, that person may have a contact here or in George's organization. Telling George now may expose that before we have a chance to find out if it goes down and what is down there."

"I get it. We'll keep it quiet until we know more." Tony smiled broadly and stepped back into the jungle, "Let's head back."

Morgan pointed back into the trees, "We need to look for a way to drive the car off to the side in the trees and away from the staging area without leaving any obvious tracks or sign that of where we went."

With that Morgan led the way back through the jungle and bush to the car where they waited for the others to start another day.

Chapter 16 - Success

The next morning they left the hotel early again and drove out to the staging site.

As Morgan drove closer, he slowed down to find a path that veered off to the right, upstream, into the jungle and trees to hide their Land Cruiser. He was looking for a way to park about a quarter or a half kilometer from the main road leading to the staging area and in a way that did not leave obvious tracks into the bush.

He found a sandy and rough side road, flanked by dense bushes, that veered off in the right direction and didn't look like it would show obvious signs of travel. He carefully, slowly drove down the rough, pot-hole filled road for several hundred meters, slowly angling toward the upstream part of the river. When the rough road became impassable they parked. They both looked around for any signs or sounds of others, only hearing the cacophony of jungle life in the background.

Morgan pulled out his small pack with a rope, sling, flashlight and 2 bottled waters. Even at this early 06:30 it was already hot and muggy. His shirt was starting to stain wet. He looked over at Tony who was already sweating and wet. Tony wrapped a pale green handkerchief around his forehead and tied it behind.

Morgan quietly closed the door and paused to take in the sounds and smells of the jungle. He was intently focused on any odd smells or noises not native to the jungle.

Tony just waited patiently knowing his friend's way of sensing the environment around them.

Morgan remained quiet, looked at Tony, nodded forward, then started to maneuver through the heavy bush and trees towards the ravine edge they had found the day before.

He stopped and smiled as Tony stepped up next to him. Still grinning, he nodded and then stepped down the old and narrow stone path into the ravine using his left hand on the wall to help balance as he began his climb down.

The gusty wind and mist were almost absent this early. The path was neither wet or slick so the footing was difficult, but not unsafe. He looked over his left shoulder at Tony who was right behind him and focused on where his feet were stepping. They continued down into the ravine and slowly, carefully made their way to the bottom. About 3 meters from the bottom the stone path ended at a jumble of boulders the size of soccer balls and bigger.

Morgan stopped to relax from the focused work of safely negotiating the down-climb.

Tony huffed out of breath from the effort, just smiled from ear to ear and quietly said, "Morg, this is just fantastic. Lead on and let's go find an airplane."

Morgan just nodded and smiled. He moved through the stones, carefully stepping over and around them then stepped onto a narrow beach at the edge of the churning river. He looked up and around. The area they were in felt like a bowl, wide at the bottom with the ravine walls narrowing toward the top. The geology was unusual, here at the bottom, the rushing river churned around the corner up against the rock wall on the other side, but left a narrow strip of beach on their side. The rock walls were sheer, smooth and would be impossible to climb.

He looked up and around then down stream toward the plane. Tony joined him and they both were just stood there stunned into silence.

The Ercoupe was 100 meters down stream and jammed into a narrow part of the ravine walls, hanging nose down, only about 7 meters above the beach and stone.

Morgan focused intently on the plane and just shook his head, "It can't be this easy. Really?"

Tony smiled broadly, "I keep saying it, you're the man. You have the gift to figure this stuff out."

Morgan looked at his watch, it was now 07:20 and the wind and mist were starting to pick up briskly. He walked across the sand covered rocks and stones to a point directly under and to one side of the small plane. It was so close he could almost touch it. He took out his smartphone and took several pictures. He tried to move behind the plane to the other side but the river had widened there and ended the little beach. It was either incredible luck or strange coincidence that the small plane had crashed into this narrow section of the ravine.

Morgan carefully climbed the rock wall supporting the right wing tip and scaled high enough to rest his hand on the aluminum wing. He looked into the canopy but was barely able to see inside, the decades of dirt and water had clouded the glazed bubble canopy. From where the wing lay on the rocky knob protrusion he had scaled, he could almost touch the fuselage. Rather than risk the injury, he carefully climbed down and just stood looking up and smiling... his brain spinning and processing their next steps.

Tony walked up next to him as Morgan examined the plane. "Look, the wings are holding it between the walls. See how it is jammed there at the wing tips on both sides?"

Tony pointed up at the cracked and curved windshield canopy. "I don't see any big holes so the stuff George wants may still be inside, if it was inside when she crashed." Tony ambled closer to Morgan, "How do we get up inside?"

Morgan continued to look at the plane, "Not today. We need to get some gear." He paused looking up at the plane then back at Tony, "We're going to need 2 radios, a painter's ladder, construction gloves, painter's masks, goggles, a canvas duffel bag, our small day pack, a dynamic climbing rope, say about 11 mm, a fully static, nylon line that can hold 3,000 pounds, a climbing harness and at some point a truck with a cable winch… maybe."

Tony chuckled, "Then maybe you have an extraction plan? Some of that stuff may be tough to get around here and certainly difficult to acquire discretely, if you know what I mean."

Morgan smiled again, "Remember Senor Martinez who rented us the Land Cruiser? He has the construction rental business, right? He may have most of this stuff and we can improvise on the climbing gear if needed, or use similar stuff he may have." Morgan turned to Tony, " It sounded like he might be willing to work with us… quietly."

Morgan paused, nodding back toward the plane, "Or, we start with the ladder, mask and goggles and do this in two phases."

Morgan began to head back and turned one last time to look at the tantalizingly close plane. He nodded back at the plane then they headed back up the stone path to their hidden SUV.

Chapter 17 - The First Recovery

Morgan sat on a rock and looked at the airplane with deep, focused concentration.

Tony asked him "What about parking a 4x4 at the top, attaching a long cable extension to a front mounted winch and dropping it down to hold you up over the plane to give you access and…"

Morgan interjected, "Give me a moment. Let me think about this." He then pondered the situation for a few minutes and then slowly got up.

"Let's find two flat rocks."

Tony cocked his head in confusion and looked at him with a questioning stare.

"Let's work with what we have here. Let's get a couple of flat rocks to take the load of my weight and the ladder and we try to gently set it against the plane. You support the ladder so that it doesn't lean or shift and I'll see if I can climb up and look inside the plane. How does that sound?"

Tony looked at him for a moment, "That sounds simple… but will it cause the plane to shift or knock it over?"

"Not if we keep the ladder almost vertical, put all the weight on the stones and keep almost no pressure on the fuselage."

He extended the long, aluminum painter's ladder up, section by section to make the length more than 7 meters.

Morgan lifted it up and carefully, gently rested the painter's extension ladder against the right side of the fuselage facing them. He and Tony then planted the larger, flatter stones on the sand directly underneath to support the feet of the ladder so they wouldn't sink in the sand and tilt the ladder out of balance.

Morgan adjusted the angle and kept a very small angle for the ladder to not apply too much pressure to the side of the small plane as he knew that Aluminum was notorious for leaching and slowly melting away, ruining its structural integrity. Also, he wasn't sure how precarious the stuck airplane was. He was careful not to put too much stress on the structure, even though it had withstood decades of storms and winds lodged and jammed between the two rock walls.

Morgan looked out at the raging river, then up into the swirling mist growing by the minute.

He put on the painters mask, goggles and gloves, buckled the carpenters tool belt around his waist with a hammer, big screw driver, pliers and a one meter long litter grabber, already secured on the belt.

Tony smiled and held the back of the ladder firmly as Morgan began his climb up.

He watched the wing and the fuselage for any sign of movement, but the plane was clearly wedged between the rock walls. He carefully continued to step up the ladder to the canopy, looked down at Tony to make sure he was holding the ladder safely and then turned to look inside the airplane cockpit at the mess.

Hanging from the seat belt was a jumble of old, shredded shirt and pants with some bones still attached, clearly the remains of Isabella Torres.

Morgan looked for a moment, with a grim, sad look. He gently shook his head to refocus and carefully grabbed a broken section of the glazed canopy from the side of the plane, being careful to not apply too much pressure to the side of the plane.

He gently tried to move it and the broken piece wiggled loose. Morgan slowly, more confidently began to work on the plane canopy to break away sections of the cracked and broken side window.

He made a hole big enough to lean into.

He looked again at the pile of remains in the foot well that was Isabella. He looked closer on his side of the plane and saw a heavily stained wood box about a 30 centimeters wide, 30 centimeters long and about 20 centimeters high, a jumble of broken bits of glass, acrylic, and 3 brown, mud covered cylinders.

With a heavy sigh and deep breath, he grabbed the windshield support bar, bent over and reached down into the foot well of the plane with the litter grabber tool.

Morgan was able to methodically tease apart and grasp each of the mud covered cylinders, pull them out using the litter grabber and place them into his carpenters pouch. The wooden box was more difficult because of the location on the floor and its size and weight. It had clearly been thrown around and showed large scrapes and chipped edges.

Morgan tried several times to reach down with the tool and grasp it but his perch on the ladder and the depth of the footwell put the box just out of reach. He stood up straight to rest his back and ponder his next step. The wind and mist were becoming very gusty and he was concerned about the added pressure on the ladder and plane.

Tony tapped on the side of the ladder and Morgan looked down. "Anything I can do to help? Need any tools or do you want to take a break?"

Morgan shook his head, "I am sooo close."

He reached back inside with the litter grabber, stretching as far as he could, to pull it up. The thin metal jaws on the front of the litter grabber began to bend as he started to pull up the box.

He heard a slight groan from the fuselage as the box started to shift position. His fear and adrenaline immediately spiked. He slowly and carefully began to pull the box up more slowly and carefully.

As he hoisted it up, he estimated the weight at about 5 kilos or so. When the box came up another foot, he held the litter grabber tool up with his right hand and carefully reached in to grab the handle of the box with his left. He smiled to himself as he pulled it out of the plane.

Carefully Morgan turned to show Tony and slowly descended the ladder to the bottom, handing the box to Tony.

Morgan stepped carefully down and then off the last ladder rung, looked up then gently pulled the ladder away from the plane. He pulled the extension rope to disengage the lock and lower the top segment of the ladder to shorten it.

He and Tony put the 3 mud covered cylinders into a large plastic bag, then stuffed them into their day pack.

Morgan looked up at the plane and rolled his head and neck to let go of the muscle stress from the tense work.

Tony placed the wood box on a flat rock and opened it. The inside was a soggy, wet mess of mud and wood chips. Under that was a wrapped canvas package, still covered in oil impregnated cloth to protect it from water and rust.

They both shrugged. "Lets keep this covered and we'll hand it over to George, whatever it is. You okay with that?"

Tony looked over at him, "I don't know what is in it but agree we let him unwrap it."

He smiled broadly at Tony, "Step one is done. Let's get upstairs and take the equipment back to Senor Martinez."

Morgan tucked the box and the wrapped documents into a narrow hole next to a large boulder. Satisfied they were hidden, they began the hike back up the thin stone path, each carrying one end of the ladder with their left hand and using their right arm on the rock wall to keep their balance. When they got to the top, they set the ladder on top of the luggage rack of the Toyota and lashed it down.

Morgan paused to listen to the jungle to see if there were changes in the constant sound of the trees swaying and the insect life buzzing. He stopped for a moment, cocking his head to one side, listening intently. Something was different, but he couldn't work it out. His intuition was trying to tell him something. The sounds were the same, the smells seemed the same and nothing seemed out of place. He shook his head with impatience to keep going, so they both headed back down the path to retrieve the box and rolled documents.

They got to the bottom. Morgan was still feeling a bit spooked. He looked around to see if there were any signs of people or other footprints. Finding none, he pulled the box and documents from behind the boulder.

Tony grinned broadly, "This is so incredible. How do you want to play this with George?"

Morgan cocked his head to one side in thought, looking at Tony and then up the winding path. "Very carefully. If you take the box up and stash it in the back under the tools and tarp, I'll clean off the rolls here at the water's edge and meet you up there in a few minutes. I just want to make sure the documents are still in good shape. And Tony, when you get back up, look around, okay? Be careful. Something just doesn't feel… right. Sound like a plan?"

"Yup, that would be perfect." Tony grabbed the box and proceeded up the trail. "I'll be careful and watch out. If I see or hear anyone, I'll come back down here. See you in a few." The gusty wind and foggy air was picking up again and his words were barely heard over the sound of the river and wind.

Morgan knelt down at the river edge and washed the oil cloth cylinders. He was careful to remove all of the mud and dirt that had accumulated from the years of exposure to the elements while inside the hanging airplane.

The oil impregnated canvas covers were still in pristine condition. He dried all of the water off of them with paper towels from his day pack and then carefully unwrapped the first roll. The paper contents were in perfect condition and still clear. It was a map of South America with a text list on one side and little flag markers on the map. The descriptions included "Gold", "Silber", "Kupfer", "Smaragd" and other words Morgan had never heard of before.

He figured it was some kind of mineral map. He shrugged then used his phone to take several detailed pictures of the map and descriptions list.

Morgan carefully rolled the paper back up in the oil skin cloth being careful to have it look exactly the way he found it and still keep it sealed by the water proof oil impregnated canvas.

Satisfied the first was done, he cleaned and unrolled the second one and carefully looked at the condition of the single typed page, not bothering to read it. He was in a hurry to get back up to the car so they could leave. He photographed it with his phone, quickly rolled it back up and wrapped it in its oil skin cover. He did the same thing with the third roll, took a picture of each page in the document then rolled it back up resealing it.

Morgan quickly put them back in the plastic bag, rolled them up to make sure there was no air inside then tucked it into his day pack for safety. He stood up and immediately started up the path, turning to look over his shoulder one last time at the small airplane as he scurried up the steep, rocky steps of the incline.

Morgan crested the edge of the ravine and moved through the bushes toward their car. As Morgan got back to their vehicle, he finally began to calm his nerves, it was finally going according to plan. He could finally relax. He tucked the small day pack with the cylinders behind and under the passenger seat, and looked for Tony.

He walked around the passenger side of the car and found Tony, face down with a bullet hole in the center of his back.

Morgan had not even heard a shot. He instantly crouched down, looking for an adversary. There was no one.

His keen hearing heard the faint sound of another car moving away through the jungle. He ran down the path they had used to drive into the jungle. He only saw the dust of a vehicle rapidly leaving the jungle, heading down the road but could not make out what kind of vehicle or who was in it. The dust was too thick, billowing about like a fog.

Morgan screamed in anger, arching his back with clenched fists. He fell to his knees, tears running down his cheeks. He was so upset he was shaking with anger and sorrow.

Tony was gone. And nothing he could do would bring him back. He had such a huge hole in his life now. His chest felt like it was going to explode. He sobbed for a moment. Morgan's heart was racing with Adrenalin, sorrow and fearsome anger. He slowly stood up and wiped the tears from his cheeks. He reached into his pocket and took out his handkerchief, wiping his face. He looked around. There was no one around and the jungle had returned to its business, the ever-present cacophony of sound and smells returned to normal.

Still very upset but feeling as though he was in a surreal mental fog, he managed to lift Tony's body into the Land Cruiser. He looked around the car for the wooden box but it was gone.

Morgan explored further into the bush looking for the missing box but didn't find it. Thinking that maybe Tony had already put it in the car, he went back to check that. The back of the Land Cruiser still held their collection of tools, ropes, masks, belts and the ladder on the roof, but no wooden box.

Morgan, began to have a sinking feeling in the pit of his stomach that who ever shot Tony, stole the box. They'd be in for a surprise to find it was just an old mechanical device and likely not worth a lot.

He slowly got into the car trying to process what had happened and trying to figure out who would do this. Was it rebels? No, that doesn't make any sense, if they had been rebels, they would have stayed and shot him, too, then stolen the car. And, they hadn't seen of or heard of rebels. Maybe someone from the team? But who would do that? No one knew what they were trying to do or that they would even be at that spot in the jungle.

He was furious and devastated at his loss. He sat still for several minutes his hands clenching the steering wheel, his face an unemotional mask hiding the seething hatred he was feeling. Morgan was trying to absorb what had happened and found no answers. His emotions kept shifting from extreme sorrow, to anger, to hatred and back to sorrow. He felt like he was in an emotional tornado.

He slowly started the car and drove to the work site.

Chapter 18 - A Fatal Setback

Morgan hurriedly drove back, his Land Cruiser bouncing over the rough ruts and roads.

George was there standing next to his car, away from the work teams, talking with his guards. The two work teams were already toiling away with their daily plans near the ravine edge to try and reach the plane. Morgan quickly looked around for rebels or some other antagonist, but saw none. The only person not immediately visible was Maria. He quickly drove up and jumped out.

Morgan brusquely interrupted their discussion, "George! Tony is dead. He was shot in the back."

George's team gathers around him, "What? What happened? Where?" George pointed toward the South, "We heard a shot in the jungle but thought is might be a hunter."

Morgan pointed to the South and into the jungle. "We found a way down into the ravine further South and were coming back up. He went back to the car before I did and was shot in the back by someone. I saw the car leave but there was so much dust, I couldn't see who it was or what kind of vehicle it was. Is everything okay here? Has anyone attacked here?"

George looked at his team and back at Morgan, "No, everything is fine here, the teams are working trying to get to the airplane. The only one not here is Maria, I have not seen her today. Are you concerned about rebels? Who else would attack us?" George's guards looked out and around for any sign or sound of an adversary, their hands pulling up their machine pistols, clicking the safeties off but leaving their fingers resting against the trigger guards.

"I don't know, I'm just trying to figure this out." Morgan sighed heavily, looked around at the work groups and then back at George.

With a confused and uncertain look, Morgan continued, "We were able to get into the plane from down below."

George's eyebrows shot up, he focused intently on Morgan and started to speak.

Morgan waived his hand to cut him off then handed him the day pack, "I think these are what you have been looking for. There are 3 rolled up documents in oil skin cloth wrapping. I cleaned off the mud and mold."

George paused, stunned at the revelation of what Morgan had just handed him, "Morgan, this is incredible… just incredible. You got them all? There are no other items?"

"No George, those are the only documents we found. Were there supposed to be more"

"No, just the three documents. Oh, hold on a minute. Wasn't there also a wooden box? Did you recover that?"

"Yes we did. I think whoever shot Tony, took the box. We opened it but it looked like some kind of mechanism wrapped in the same kind of oilskin for the documents. We never opened it up. What is it?"

George responded "I don't know. I only know there was a wood box with a mechanical device in it."

Morgan exploded, "How are we going to find out who did this? Someone killed my friend and we need to find them. Now!"

George calmly responded. "How? How do we do that? We don't have any idea who shot at you or who was in the vehicle that left when you found Tony."

"I don't know how, you are the spook, you have access to the intelligence network, you figure it out. He isn't just some casualty of this operation, we need to find and deal with the people who killed him."

Morgan was furious, waving his hands around and moving from side to side venting his anger.

A bullet ripped through his left leg. followed by several seconds of silence and then a loud cracking boom sound. Morgan instantly knew it was a sniper round as the force of the impact of the bullet shoved him against George knocking him over. Another round whistled past George's head striking a guard in the ribs, easily piercing the side of his bullet proof vest and knocking him over. He doubled over in pain with the glancing wound breaking two of his right ribs.

Two other guards quickly covered George. The fourth guard was already running as fast as he could down the brush covered, dirt road weaving through cover toward the distant position of the sniper.

The Brag team was also on their stomachs, slowly shimmying their way over toward George, his guards and Morgan.

George tightly clutched the small day pack carrying the 3 rolled documents. He looked over at the approaching Brag team, the other workers hunched down and whispered fiercely, "Morgan. Do not tell anyone about this. This is secret. That guy who attacked you in the alley worked for Senator Cole. It looks like he is trying to get these documents for his own use. So, don't discuss these with the work team or Brag squad, or anyone else. Am I clear?"

Morgan simply nodded, still stunned by the bleeding shot to his left leg, stunned by the long distance rifle attack and still reeling in disbelief his friend was gone.

Later, Morgan met with George back at the hotel after an embassy medic had driven out to the hotel to clean and sew Morgan's gun shot wound and to take the injured guard back to be treated by an American doctor who would not ask questions about the injury.

Morgan gently rubbed the newly sewn wound. It still leaked through the fresh bandage and slightly stained his new pants. Morgan looked distantly out the hotel window processing what had happened to Tony and since then. The only one unaccounted for was Maria, but he had difficulty believing she would shoot them. Then he remembered the gun case in the back of her SUV. Before he could say anything George interrupted his deep thought.

George looked at Morgan solemnly, "Did you read them? Do you know what they are?"

"No, I didn't. I cleaned them up but did not read them."

"Morgan, how do I know you are telling me the truth?"

"We didn't have time to read them, we were so concerned to make sure they were well sealed and in good shape before we turned them over to you that I looked at the paper to make sure it was dry and in good shape, then rolled them back up to give them to you. If you doubt my word, I'll take a lie detector test if you prefer."

George softened, "No need for that, I believe you. And, thank you very much. You likely saved my life today." George changed the subject, "Tony was right, you do have great skill at finding planes and figuring out how to get into them and recover them. Just look at the men who died in the work team and the Brag squad trying to figure out how to get to the plane."

Morgan pulls his head up from his hands covering his face, "Well, we're not done yet. It is still down there, so I haven't recovered it yet."

"I need to leave for the embassy. I'll be back late tonight in case you need to contact me. I want to send the documents with a courier as soon as I can to get them back home. There is someone there I know I can trust to take them back into the U. S. and not let them get taken. How are you planning to recover the plane?"

Morgan looked over at him not wanting to share the idea forming in his mind, "I don't know yet, I'm working on it."

Morgan couldn't bear to go back to the work site, so he sat down in the lobby to process what had happened and to think about Tony.

He paused to clear his mind of his grief and to focus on the next task. He pulled a business card out of his pocket and made a phone call.

Chapter 19 - The Second Recovery

Morgan and Luis Martinez, Alejandro Martinez's son, carefully removed the aged remains and clothes of Isabella Elena Torres from the seat and foot well of the plane using the same litter grabber tool as before, carefully placing the bones and shredded clothes into the white cotton, cloth bag Alejandro Martinez provided.

Morgan reached down the ladder and carefully, respectfully, handed it to Alejandro who held the light weight bag with reverence, closed his eyes for a moment in silent prayer, crossed himself and then gently set it down next to their gear. He turned to look at Morgan and quietly said, "Thank you." Morgan saw his words, but could not hear them over the rush of the raging river.

Morgan turned back to the plane and wrapped a thick, nylon lifting belt around the Ercoupe. He handed the end to Luis on the other side of the plane and received the loop ends back from him.

He clipped the hanging cable from above to the four loop ends and signaled to Senor Martinez below, 'thumb up'.

They both climbed down their ladders and pulled them carefully away from the fuselage.

Senor Martinez was already talking in the radio and quietly gesturing with his hands toward the airplane and the sky far above them.

They pulled the latches and their ladders retracted back to their folded size. They both moved the ladders away to the rocky side next to the ravine wall and out from under the plane.

The mist and gusty wind were just starting to pick up, swirling around them and beginning to build a heavy mist. Morgan was unsure if his plan would be successful but knew their time was running out… quickly. It was now or never to retrieve the plane. With years of practiced ease, he stepped back to quickly look over their set up. Satisfied they were as ready as they would ever be, he twirled his left index finger in the air for Alejandro to tell the winch operator to start pulling the cable up.

On queue the steel cable tightened up and Senor Martinez cautioned them to stop. the cable slack was gone and the under-wing lifting straps were in perfect position.

Morgan looked up at the crumpled plane and then over to Senor Martinez, lifting his index finger up, slowly twirling it for the winch operator to proceed.

Senor Martinez spoke again, gesturing with his hand back and forth like an orchestra conductor.

Everyone watched intently as the cable began to pull more tightly against the fragile, damaged aluminum frame. An ominous creaking and groaning noise began to get louder and louder over the sound of the rushing river. With a final, loud crack, the plane popped up a foot from its precarious perch where it had rested all of these decades.

Morgan raised his hand, palm out, then closed his fingers into a fist to signal Alejandro to stop lifting. Senor Martinez quickly and emphatically spoke into the radio, the river drowning out the sound for Morgan and Luis.

Morgan walked back over near the plane and waited. After a minute the swirling, gusts began to affect the plane and it started a slow spin. As the wings turned even with the river flow, Morgan looked over to Senor Martinez and signaled to lower the airplane by slowly twirling his left index finger down.

He and Luis cautiously walked over to the airplane as it slowly descended and they each reached up, grabbed the wings to guide it over the sand, pushing the small airplane away from the river. The nose and broken propeller settled into the rocky, sandy beach. They both pushed the wings harder to force the weight and center of gravity back towards the rock wall and away from the torrent river.

Morgan pushed on the wing with one hand and used the other to signal Senor Martinez for the winch operator to continue to lower the cable down. Alejandro transmitted that through the radio constantly updating the winch operator at the top of the ravine on their status. The airplane settled flat onto the beach, nose in the sand and tail on the boulders near the wall - the first time it had been on flat land since before it crashed.

Morgan and Senor Martinez just smiled.

Senor Martinez walked over as Morgan was un-clipping the lifting belt. Alejandro spoke one last time into the radio and the lifting cable soared up the ravine wall and disappeared above them.

"Senor Fox, thank you so very much for retrieving our Isabella and helping us to bring down her plane. Next week we will continue from here to quietly remove the wings and pull it up the cliff to our shipping container."

"You are very welcome Senor Martinez. I am glad it worked out. I'd appreciate it if we did not share how we pulled it out."

"We won't. I would be worried that others may try to steal it or confiscate it. This is our shrine to Isabella and her father. We will find a very good and secret place to place it where only our family can view it." Alejandro stepped in front of Morgan, "If you ever need anything from us, please do not hesitate to contact us. We owe you so very much for this feat and the closure you bring to our lost family."

Morgan looked out over the raging torrent of river and up into the heavy swirling mist fogging up and completely hiding the top of the ravine. "It must be nearing time for the others to arrive."

"Do not worry, Luis has already left and will move the truck into the trees away from the site so that he won't be discovered. There is no rush now, we can hide the truck and bring it back later. We'll pick him up in our company van along the main road when we travel home."

Morgan thought for a moment, cocking his head to one side, "Are you concerned at all for rebels stealing your truck?"

Alejandro looked over with a slightly puzzled look, "There are no rebels in this part of Venezuela. We are fortunate that we don't need to worry about that."

Chapter 20 - A Surprise Awaits

Monday morning brought the teams together at the operation site as they usually did.

They all began to set up and the Brag team began their first daily descent into the chaotic swirling fog and gusty, turbulent wind. An hour into the down-climb the lead Army Ranger, heard a call on his radio.

"What, say that again?" He looked up at the sky, focused on the radio and rolled his eyes. They had failed. They were too late, the airplane was no longer there and had apparently, finally, succumbed to the elements having fallen into the river to be destroyed by the torrential river, falls and boulders down stream.

He was both relieved, frustrated and disappointed at the failure that had cost the lives of half his team.

He asked again for visual confirmation of the message. When it came back strongly affirming the plane was now gone, he instructed the Master Sargent to pull up the climber.

Once that started, he walked over to George and one of the Hispanic workers arguing over the next steps in their retrieval plan. Maria had not returned to the work site and no one knew where she had vanished to. That left George trying to communicate and interpret what the worker was saying. He spoke English but it was a struggle to fully understand him.

The Lieutenant interrupted them, "The plane is gone. My climber got as far as we did on Friday. Friday he could see the tail of the plane and outline of it. Today, he can see parts of the river below. It looks like it finally deteriorated enough to collapse into the river."

George acted upset and hugely disappointed. He rolled his eyes and turned his head to the sky in mock disgust at the loss, "Really? Is there any chance he is wrong and the mist is hiding it?"

"No. He said he could just make out the river below, between the two sides of the ravine and could not see any sign of the plane. 'Sorry, sir."

George conferred with the Lieutenant and the Hispanic team leader for a few more minutes and then nodded, put his hand up to pause the discussion. "Do either of you feel there is a chance to find the plane downstream?"

They both looked at each other then back at George and shook their heads.

The Lieutenant added, "It would be harder to get to it than this is and the plane would have broken up in the fall downstream and across the waterfalls."

George sighed heavily and just nodded grimly, "Call the teams together, let's get this closed up."

George brought all of the teams together, "In case you have not heard the news, the plane is no longer hanging in the ravine. We speculate that it finally collapsed into the river and has been carried downstream or over the falls. After discussing our options with your team leads, I am going to close down our retrieval effort. If the plane has fallen into the river, it will have been torn apart by the falls and rocks. There won't be anything left to recover of the pilot or any belongings she may have had. Let's pack it up and close down the site. Thank you all for your hard work, it just didn't end as we hoped it would."

He paused thoughtfully, "I will discuss our loss with the people who hired us." With that he turned to the Hispanic team lead and Lieutenant, "I am going to head back to wrap up from the hotel. Please close up the site and make sure it is cleaned up. I'll contact both of you when we get back to cover any loose ends. Okay?"

They both simply nodded stoically with nothing further to say, turned and strode off toward their respective teams and vehicles.

Chapter 21 - A Dire Turn

Morgan was bone tired and weary from the ordeal of trying to solve how to get into the plane and recover it. He was emotionally exhausted and angry at Tony's death, angry at his personal loss, frustrated, confused and feeling sorry for himself with no idea how to avenge Tony's death and no idea how to go on, once he got home.

He stopped and tried to really wrap his head around it, that his close friend and mentor was gone. His eyes blurred a bit and he blinked them rapidly to take the tears away.

It was just so horrible. And, he thought, horrible as well for the Venezuelan workers and U. S. Army members that had died. Yes, but Tony was gone.

He looked vacantly out the window not really paying attention to what was going on in the street outside, just letting his brain be numb. His leg was now throbbing from the pain where he'd been shot.

His phone rang in his pocket. He pulled it out and looked at the number. It was George Bolton. His face tightened up, shaking his head in disgust, 'What now…' he thought as he tapped the phone, "George."

George spoke loudly on the other end, "Morgan, I have another problem. Well actually, WE have a problem."

"No George, YOU have a problem. My best friend was just killed and my wife is divorcing me, I have no idea how to piece my life back together. What can be worse than that. I'm getting on an airplane in… about 2 hours and heading home. I need to talk with my wife to see if we can mend our marriage."

"Morgan, did you read those documents?"

"I TOLD you I didn't read them! Why don't you believe me? If needed, I would swear that under oath. Why do you keep asking that?"

"Okay, okay, I believe you. Are you alone and in a quiet place? No one else around?"

"Yes George, I'm sitting in the hotel lobby and am the only one here. Why? What the hell is going on?"

George paused to frame his thoughts, "I was going to ship the documents through the diplomatic courier at the embassy. I showed the ambassador the two documents still in German. I don't speak German and thought he might help me quickly get a read on what they were. One was a map of the country that showed high quality mineral deposits. The other document has created… an emergency we need to take care of."

"What is that?"

"The family who fled Germany at the end of the war brought many stolen items including a secret treaty, a map and a German nuclear weapon."

"Come on George that isn't even funny. If Germany had the 'bomb' during the war they would have won. We'd all be speaking German now."

"Yes except it wasn't finished until right before the war ended. They never had a chance to use it. Fortunately, we built ours first and the war ended. Otherwise they would have nuked a city, maybe even London. That they didn't deploy it leaves us with the extreme problem we have now."

"George, how do you even know there is a bomb? Where did they put it and how could it be used now?"

"Morgan, you gave me three documents. The first document was the key document we were concerned about, the second document was the map with areas of rich mineralization. The third document the ambassador translated for me was the instruction on how to use the mechanical detonator to set off the bomb. It described the detonator as being stored in a wooden box with metal handles on either side. The detonator itself was wrapped in oil skin cloth to protect the finely machined interior clock work from rust and corrosion. It described the box as about a foot wide, a foot long and a half a foot high. Sound familiar?"

"Okay, so the box in the plane MAY have been the detonator and it was stolen, but how would they know what it was or how to use it, or even where the bomb was.

"Morgan, there are port records that show that when Generalmajor Schmid arrived here with his family, one of the items was large. They described it as the size of a car and very heavy, so they thought it was a car. The records show it was taken away on a flat bed type cargo truck. He may have brought the weapon here. I have a team looking for Schmid and his relatives."

"Schmid… Schmid? I know that name."

"From where, Morgan? This is really important, where did you hear that name?"

"Not 'hear' it, but 'read' it. Tony and I were talking with Maria…"

George interrupted him, "Maria? As in Maria Lopez?"

Morgan continued smoothly, "Yes, as in your Maria. She had the back hatch of her SUV open and we looked inside. at the back were towels, a dirty blanket, other stuff and a hard case."

George interrupted again, "A hard case?"

"Yeah, a rifle case that was old and battered. Just above the leather handle was a brass name plate that said 'Schmid'. That is where I know the name. Your Maria is a Schmid or knows one."

George visibly winced, "She is not my Maria. I want to check up on that now. I'll call you later, for now, do NOT get on that plane. I need you here."

"Why me, I don't know anything about bombs, certainly not… 75 year old German nuclear weapons."

"Maybe not, but the Brag team already shipped out and any other team who might be able to help us are thousands of miles away. You are my best chance to get this. Tony was absolutely right, you have a gift for finding and fixing. Stay put. I'll call you later."

Chapter 22 - Revelation

George interrupted Morgan, "After Maria disappeared we started an inquiry to find her and found out she has been in contact with German and Russian members of their embassies trying to negotiate the sale of a very old, top secret document that would be embarrassing to the United States. When we learned that, we did a full work up."

Morgan looked confused, "George, how would she even know about all of that stuff?"

"We looked into her family and her last name is Lopez after her father and her mother's maiden name is Schmid."

"I got that from the gun case. But how would she know about the document, or the detonator or the bomb."

"We are speculating she may have learned about it from some family document or diary. But that is speculation. Her first attempted contact looks like it was just before you both were involved and I know I didn't tell her or discuss this with anyone locally. So, my team is thinking there is a family document that describes what was brought over from Germany. That is the current consensus anyway."

"Okay, so, she stole the detonator to sell the package since she didn't get the documents? I don't understand what she is doing, George. Does she know where the bomb is? And then how can she move it. It may have been easy in 1945 to run around the countryside with a nuclear weapon but now a days aren't there things, like radiation detectors that would pinpoint it?"

"There are, but not here. And our current assessment indicates that isn't likely her goal. Based on her history and her family, she may have stolen the detonator to some how use the package to exact some kind of revenge."

"Use it, why, what possible sense does that make?"

"Our sources say her family, post-war, tried to buy their way into the local elite and shipping business with a very poor outcome. They were ostracized and treated… poorly. Maria has a lot of questionable activities and violent behavior in her background. Both of those together may indicate some potential desire to get even."

"Okay, then… if they have the bomb, if she has the bomb, they would have needed a place to store it. Do the Schmid family still own any property?"

"We are already looking at that. The only thing we've found so far is a small abandoned warehouse down at the harbor in Maracaibo."

"How the hell do you know it is abandoned?"

"We, uh… re-tasked a satellite to take a look…"

"I do NOT believe this crap." Morgan interrupted shaking his head. He paused, then added, "What is the address and I'll start there, then."

"Morgan, I'll get you the address. Just so you know, Maracaibo is a big city, and the harbor connects Lake Maracaibo to the Gulf of Venezuela and the Caribbean Sea. It is also the prime center of their oil industry."

"So, George, let me see. What are you saying here, that there is some urgency?"

"Yes and Maracaibo has about two and a half million people.

"Send me the address, I'll go look."

"Great, glad you'll do it."

"Not sure I have a choice here. You canceled my airline reservation and shared that, oh by the way Maria may detonate a 75 year old nuclear weapon before I fly out again. Yeah, I think I need to figure this out or at least try before we all die."

"If you find her, be very careful. We did a full work up on her and she has a violent past. When she was thirteen she was bullied and taunted by a group of wealthier kids, three girls and two boys. We know that from the school records of the incident. We thought it was interesting and might shed some light on her personality, so we looked for the other kids involved to interview them. Morgan, we tracked them all down. Four of them are dead and died viciously about 10 years later. The two boys were castrated BEFORE they were killed according to the autopsy records. The 3 women were tied up, brutally beaten and two of them died. The third is in a mental hospital. To this day, she screams all day and all night at the masked person who cut her up, cut her face and gouged out her left eye."

"Okay, George... I'll be careful. I really hope I find her before she detonates the bomb."

"Morgan, thank you, but I didn't say she was going to blow everything up. That is only one of the options she has."

"Yes you did. You said your team feels her goal may be to get even. Look George, that is what my gut says. One thing Tony always said is to trust my gut. Look at it this way. She took the detonator, killed Tony, and may have shot me and tried to kill you, then disappeared with a device that can detonate a bomb after her entire family was ostracized over the last 75 years by the local aristocracy. And, she has a history of violent retribution. What does she have to lose? Nothing. What does she have to gain? Revenge! Yeah, I think she's going to use it."

Morgan paused, turning to face him, then added, "And George? I'll need a weapon."

Chapter 23 - Girding

Morgan finished cleaning the Glock 19 and tapped the 9x19 clip gently on the table to settle the bullets at the back of the clip.

His phone buzzed so he set the pistol down, picked up his phone and looked at the number. It said 'Unknown Number'. He squinted his eyes for a second and frowned as he tapped the accept button. "Hello."

George Bolton responded, "Morgan I have the address you wanted. I'll text it to you."

Morgan paused for a moment, "Okay, will you be there to take possession?"

George texted back, "No, I'll send a team. I'm here in DC arranging for one now."

Morgan, smiled. That meant George likely took the red-eye and was back in Virginia, "So, how do I disarm it, who's going to do that?"

George responded, "Check you email for instructions. We think these will work."

Morgan became more worried, "Wait, wait, you want me to try and disarm a one of a kind, 75 year old German nuclear weapon with instructions you THINK will work?"

"Morgan, it is the best we can do for you at this point. It is our best guess based on the instructions we translated."

Morgan ended, "You were smart to head home."

He abruptly disconnected the call in disgust before George could respond.

He stood up, looked at the warehouse address in the phone, put it back in his pocket and tucked the Glock behind his back, inside his belt and made sure his shirt tail hung over it. He grabbed his LED head lamp and shook his head in disappointment as he headed out the door… 'just like Afghanistan'.

Chapter 24 - Finding The Bomb

Morgan slipped through the chained corrugated metal gate still favoring his wounded left leg and looked around for anyone.

No one was inside the compound that he could see, but then he was still jittery since he hadn't seen her before she shot him in the leg, even though that was a distance shot. Well, he now assumed it was Maria who shot him. She had had the gun case in her car. She was part of the family with the bomb. She had the violent history. He frowned tight-lipped for a moment, yeah, he was pretty sure she was the sniper.

He pulled out the Glock from his waist band holding it with both hands, loosely pointed up. He moved along the edge of the wall toward the warehouse, making his way along the wall constantly scanning for movement.

There were piles of pallets that would provide convenient cover but no signs of Maria or anyone else. No sounds from inside the compound or the warehouse building. He could hear work and workers in the businesses on the other sides of the common walls, but not inside. He sniffed experimentally, but found no odd or unusual smells either to indicate any peril.

He limped into the open warehouse door, ducked inside to the right and swept the area with his gun, looking for anyone who might attack. No one was inside that he could immediately see.

Light filtered through the large glass windows at the top of the walls giving the inside space an eerie twilight feel.

His eyes adjusted quickly. No one was there. He looked around and saw that it was completely empty save the small piles of debris and dust scattered all over the large warehouse floor.

There were no large crates or other containers that would be big enough to hold a 'car sized' bomb, so he quietly stepped through and around the debris toward the obvious office set near the center of the large, open floor.

He looked down and saw faint scuff marks of someone's foot prints. He instantly dropped to his right knee, gun outstretched toward the office area, listening intently for any sound. Pain screamed up his thigh from the gun shot wound. He pushed the pain out and focused on the offices and any movement.

He scanned side to side to let his peripheral vision pick up any potential movement in the warehouse or the dark offices.

After a moment, he slowly got up and continued forward toward the offices, generally following the light scuff prints in the dust on the floor.

Still limping, he held the Glock up with two hands as he approached from the side wall and peered in. There was nothing there. He looked over the offices. Glass windows covered 3 of the 4 walls from waist high up to the office ceiling. He grimaced slightly from the pain in his leg. Clearly there was no 'car sized' object inside, just the offices and the solid back wall. Morgan began to doubt this as the spot. There was no obvious thing big enough to be the German weapon.

In his heart, his intuition told him she would use the detonator… and sooner than later. His heart pounded with the Adrenalin in his system.

He rolled around to his left side with the Glock slightly raised up. He moved slowly, still favoring his left leg and went toward the back of the office wall. He cautiously looked around the back, no one was there, he looked around the back of the warehouse wall and didn't see any large crates or doors. Again, he was disappointed, feeling he was missing something. His intuition was screaming alarms in his head. He examined the brick wall at the back of the offices, but that clearly wasn't wide enough to house a car inside.

He continued his examination around the back wall of the offices and stopped short when he saw the air vent.

Clearly there was no bomb sized room or office or crate stored here. He lowered his gun in disgust. He had failed. There were no other doors around the perimeter of the building. He grimaced again feeling they had the wrong building. The bomb was not here. He looked up into the tall rafters and around the inside of the roof. More glass windows helped to bring in thin streams of daylight. Nothing was here, but his inside intuition kept pushing him on, he was missing something.

He looked down at the dusty ground and paused. Who ever had come in, perhaps Maria, had stopped here and clearly stepped around a lot. He could see a path of footprints coming in and out, looking like the path had been used several times.

He sidled over toward the vent and the open wood box on the floor and examined it. All of the dusty floor was disturbed here. The person had spent a lot of time.

He pulled out his LED head lamp and used it as a small flashlight to look at and around the box. Someone had spent a lot of time here. He looked around the other side and the dust was untouched. He went back to the left side of the box. The only thing here was the brick wall and air vent.

He began to examine the air vent, his head lamp revealed the outline of the lever. He tried to slide it, but it didn't work. He began to fiddle more with moving it, then pushed it in and slid it. It moved and he unlocked the vent cover.

He used his headlamp to look inside. It opened up and he could see the short vent with slight scuffs in the light dust on the floor.

Morgan stopped, put the lamp down and carefully scanned the warehouse for movement or sound. There was none, so he tucked the Glock behind his back again, put the headlamp on then climbed up and into the vent. His left thigh continued screaming in discomfort. He shimmied into the vent and stood up to almost full height. He reached back behind him and quietly, carefully re-locked the vent cover. He then turned, pulled the Glock out and proceeded down the very short tunnel and around the corner.

He smiled for just a moment when he saw the stairs giving him just a glimmer of hope.

He slowly, carefully moved down the stairs with a limp, one hand on the wall for support and the other with the Glock pointed down the stairs, slowly turning his head, side to side so his head lamp would cover the basement.

At the bottom he began to scan the interior of the large sized basement. It was completely empty.

He quietly looked to his right and saw that the brick wall had apparently caved in.

Then he had an epiphany… 'caved into what?'

He hobbled over to the wall and looked into the opening and into the small room beyond. He moved his head left and right for his LED lamp to light the space.

As he stepped over the edge of the wall, he could see the canvas covered bomb to his left. It was easily as big as a car. He wondered for a moment how they would have gotten it into the basement and concluded, the basement and offices were built into the warehouse and it was set in during the construction.

He looked over the area around the canvas cover and at the back looking for traps or sensors. There were none.

He gently lifted the canvas cover exposing the metal case cover and latch. He opened it and immediately saw and heard the gently whirring of the timer. It was active and was counting down from 38 minutes, showing 00:38:17.

A cold chill went down his spine and his adrenaline began to shoot up.

He mentally went through the steps again to disable the detonator and turn off the bomb. It wasn't complicated, according to George and his team, he just had to make sure that under no circumstances could the clock numbers count down to zero while it was still attached to the bomb.

According to George, they assumed the intent of the detonator was to be a simple, unsophisticated device to just set and go. So, they assumed, there likely wouldn't be any tricks or traps.

He looked at the detonator latches and slowly turned them counter-clockwise to unscrew them.

Morgan tried to lift it out but it wouldn't budge. It was machined so carefully, it was set flush into the face of the mount.

He quickly looked over his right shoulder to make sure no one was there, then tucked the Glock back into his waist belt and grabbed two of the four latches as tightly as he could and yanked them up. The detonator lifted slowly and smoothly. He pressed it against the metal side then tucked his fingers under the edge of the device and grasped it pulling it out completely.

On the back was a thick, black, cable of wires with a special metal plug. It looked like it had 16 wires of different thicknesses or gauges going into it.

He grabbed that firmly and pulled the plug out. The timer kept ticking but was no longer connected.

He closed the metal cover on the bomb and heard a shifting, creaking noise.

He started to turn and began to grab for his gun as the brick wall behind him came crashing down shoving him to the ground and covering him in brick.

Morgan lay stunned, pinned under the brick and badly bruised up.

Of all the bad timing for the old brick wall to fail, he grimaced and thought. 'Just my luck.'

He sighed and was thankful he was still alive. His right hand was still holding the detonator off to his side. He slowly turned his head to look to his right, still covered by brick, mortar and dust.

He instantly froze when he saw the shadow moving in and quickly realized the wall hadn't failed, it was pushed. Maria was here.

He peered from under the rubble.

Maria stepped over the fallen wall behind him, "Stupid American" He quickly closed his eyes keeping his left eye a thin slit to see what she would do.

She peered at him and smiled. "Muerte! Bueno."

Maria knelt down and carefully pulled the dusty detonator from his grasp, blew the dust off of it, checked the timer to make sure it was still going.

She carefully plugged the cable connector back in and set the timer back into the case opening, turning the locking screws and closing the door.

Morgan looked up at her. She turned to look at him and was surprised to realize he was still alive. She grabbed at her belt for her revolver.

Morgan grabbed for a broken brick and threw it up at her face.

She wasn't quick enough and it hit the side of her face causing her to flinch. She fired quickly at him and the deafening noise exploded in the small space.

The bullet ricocheted off the bricks covering him, she move to aim again, this time at his head.

Morgan grabbed a handful of mortar chunks and flung it up to distract her as she fired again missing his head.

He continued moving to roll the broken bricks and mortar off his back.

She panicked again and fired too quickly, the bullet skimmed his scalp just above and behind his right ear.

He winced but kept moving his right hand behind his back, pulling the Glock out. Her gun clicked on an empty chamber. Morgan pulled and fired. His frantic and painful aim resulted in a lucky chest shot, the 9 mm round struck her in the upper left causing her to spin.

She stumbled back and quickly pulled a bayonet out with her right hand, her eyes fierce with a crazed expression. She was fighting for her life and her need for vengeance. She screamed at him and attacked with animal like ferocity, the knife point forward.

Morgan still lay on the broken bricks of the wall, leaned back and fired again hitting her center mass.

Maria was thrust back again from the shot and didn't move.

He stayed focused on her and slowly, painfully got up, physically broken.

His back was a mass of intense pain, he'd been shot and he didn't want to make the mistake again. He reached her position and could see the open eyes and dead look. The bullet had cored her sternum. He paused for a moment to slowly turn around to see if there was anyone else. There wasn't.

With a strong sigh of relief, Morgan tucked the Glock back into his belt. That was the wrong thing to do as his lower back screamed. He immediately took the Glock out and put it in his front waist band, then turned back to the bomb.

He opened the case and looked at the timer, shocked, then looked again.

She had changed the time and it now showed 00:00:12 and was counting down.

Morgan quickly unscrewed the four locking screws and again tried to pull it out. This time it was much harder. He hurt so much and he was so drained he had little strength left. He struggled to pull it out.

His adrenaline immediately exploded and he pulled as hard as he could, it creaked out from the case. He grabbed the cable connector and pulled it out of the back of the detonator. He flipped the detonator over as the time clicked past 00:00:04.

He watched the timer click down. When it hit zero, there was an audible click inside as some set of relays connected.

It then stopped and was inert.

Morgan did not realize he had been holding his breath the whole time and gasped for air. It was done, the bomb was disarmed and Maria was dead.

He thought to himself, 'My luck is not that good. Make damn sure there isn't anything else.'

He tried to straighten up and his back screamed, he had a huge headache and his whole body felt like one big bruise. He touched the side of his head and felt the gash and the blood draining from the graze.

He slowly worked his way to the side of the bomb and looked for any other wires or devices. There were none.

He slowly crawled, half stumbled over to her body to confirm she was dead.

Morgan set the device down. He pulled his phone out and saw that he had no signal and gently shook his head in disappointment.

He slowly turned to go back up the stairs and then stopped, moved his head back, looking up at the ceiling and rolled his eyes in disgust at his stupidity. He carefully maneuvered around back to the bomb, grabbed the detonator and took it with him as he slowly made his way back to the vent and the ground floor of the warehouse.

He limped and half crawled out the front of the warehouse, taking him almost a half hour to make it slowly out the warehouse door.

He pulled his phone, saw that he had a signal and texted George "Bomb disarmed Maria dead."

George instantly texted back, "Great news."

Morgan looked out at the noon day sun and the hot yard in front of the warehouse.

His phone buzzed again, he looked at it. George had texted him again, "Pull the detonator."

Morgan smiled and gently shook his head in surprise then texted back, "Already done."

George responded quickly, "Thank you".

Morgan half sat and half laid down on a small stack of pallets trying to gather the strength to walk out. He paused just soaking up the air, the smells, the sights and the feeling of still being alive, as painful as that was.

He started to get up and stopped. What's the rush, he could take the time to let his body settle a bit then try and get a taxi.

His phone buzzed again. It was George calling him. He pressed the accept button.

"Your phone shows you aren't moving. Are you okay?"

Morgan momentarily became angry at the realization of the surveillance, then quickly calmed down. Now, he was pleased and it made sense George would do that. He chuckled "I could use a medic and a ride."

George quickly responded, "The embassy team is on their way, stay put. I need to advise the President you were successful." And, ended the call.

Chapter 25 - New Eyes

Three months later, Morgan painfully limped with his crutch into a cold and empty home, he gently rubbed his lower back where the surgeon had fused three vertebrae.

He would always have the scar on his head and the round scars on his left thigh where a rifle bullet had passed through.

He felt comfortable being home. He kept thinking about his home and how much he'd missed it every single day in the hospital. He also thought about Tony a lot and decided to try and extend his fledgling and clearly failing business to include salvage. He would start a salvage tradition to remember Tony fondly every time he salvaged a plane.

His cell phone rang with a number that showed as "Unknown Number". He sadly shook his head and tapped the accept button.

"Morgan, this is George. I just wanted to say thanks for saving my life AND not blowing up Maracaibo. Your country is grateful for your service and contribution… in ways you'll never be able to learn about."

"So, there was more to it than the bomb. What was the WW2 document that we recovered."

"I can't talk about that."

"George, fuck that. I deserve to know. Tony is dead because of all of this crap. We pulled those documents out for you. One was a mineral map, you said, one was the detonator instructions, what was the other one for?"

George paused for several seconds. Morgan just let him process and didn't push him further.

"Okay, Morgan. You are right, Tony gave his life to help us safely retrieve the document. This is classified above Top Secret and must remain so."

"Understood."

"In 1939 President Franklin Delano Roosevelt and Prime Minister Neville Chamberlain signed a treaty with Adolf Hitler to give him Europe in exchange for not attacking Great Britain or the United States. You recovered the last remaining copy of that treaty"

"We did what? We 'gave' him Europe? George, that wasn't ours to give... what the hell was going on? Were we fucking crazy?"

"Morgan, it was our misguided way of trying to protect our ally and our own country." George continued, "It was an act of desperation by two world leaders who knew their countries weren't ready." He paused to gather his thoughts, "We weren't ready to go to war, our people weren't ready to go to war. We didn't have the factories set up, nor did we have the political or social 'will' to go to war. If we had gone to war then, it would have TORN America apart."

"So, what changed that? Pearl Harbor?"

"Yes, Pearl Harbor change it. That and Adolf Hitler extended his Blitzkrieg to attack England anyway. That action terminated the agreement. Apparently, Roosevelt burned his copy of the treaty. We assume Chamberlain did the same. That just left the German copy. We received an encoded communique from Ambassador Torres before he was killed that he had acquired the German copy. Then when he was murdered and we learned about his daughter's crash we realized what she was carrying. We searched for years, well, actually, over a decade... but never found it... until now. Now you know what you recovered and the reason it was so very important we receive it and not let it out."

"George, this is just crazy that we would do that. I assume our European allies do not know of the existence of the treaty?"

"No and they can never know about it. That is why we had to get to it first and not let it get out or be sold."

Morgan processed what he had heard, "Of course I'll keep it quiet."

George changed the subject, "Morgan, Tony has no next of kin, so I transferred $500,000 to your checking account and have mailed a certified letter to your home that states the money is tax free for both you and your wife. It is signed by the President. With all you have been through, I think that is fair. Again, Morgan, thank you. I have to go now. I am late for a cabinet meeting. Good bye."

As he hung up, he looked out through the broad expanse of glass and wood at the gorgeous, warm mountain day.

He grimaced at the thought he still had 4 months of Physical Therapy in front of him.

He looked through the stack of mail at all the bills. He was surprised to see a postcard from Venezuela. He turned it over and saw a short note from Tony.

He blinked back the tears in his eyes and read the note.

"Morgan, I know we are deep in the middle of this here, but wanted to send you this short note for later. You really do have a gift. Don't focus on what you don't have, focus on what you do have. I read this quote from George Bernard Shaw, an Irish playwright and thought of you. *People are always blaming their circumstances for what they are. I don't believe in circumstances. The people who get on in this world are the people who get up and look for the circumstances they want, and, if they can't find them, they make them.* Morgan, you should do the same. -- Best, T "

Morgan nodded at the sentiment and smiled. He painfully limped with his cane out on his back deck and carefully eased his butt into a cushioned patio chair to just take in the broad, beautiful expanse of rolling hills, the forests and the incredible pine wood scent. He was home.

Thank you for reading my story. If you have time, please leave a review. If you would like to read more stories, please check out my books, fan art and sign up for my newsletter at JTSkye.com

Printed in Great Britain
by Amazon